A Good Snowy Winter

Tiana Or-Gordon

Published by Or-Gordon Enav – Linterin Books

2017

First Edition

10 9 8 7 6 5 4 3 2 1

Edited by Fritz Rickhoff

Cover painting and graphic design by Vlada Shamova

Illustrated by Agáta Motlochová

First Online Publishing: Kindle Direct Publishing

ISBN: 978-80-907066-1-3 (Kindle)

Printed by CreateSpace, an Amazon.com Company

Available from Amazon.com (First Printing)

ISBN: 978-80-907066-0-6

FOR MY PARENTS

CONTENTS

Open your eyes,

Look around.

Now close them,

Forget everything.

Let all your thoughts disappear one by one

And come back by imagining.

There's nothing around you

Until you find it,

You're the one who designed lands and ocean.

You are the king, you are the subject,

Reality's based on your notion.

Keep your eyes closed

For a little longer…

Then open them once again.

Is what you see the same thing I observe?

Is this the world we deserve?

GOLDEN APPLES

Idunn lived in a small village near the mountains. She didn't know very much about the world beyond the walls of the high cliffs. It took almost a week to get to the other side by car and then another few hours by airplane. Idunn never needed to leave this small and lovely place, she was content. However, the people here couldn't live without some disagreements or troubles, and so it happened, that strange rumors began to spread throughout the village.

The neighbors started talking about a new cave, found in the mountains. They mentioned something about dark magic and Idunn stopped reading to listen in on their conversations.

"This young man, who is teaching biology in the school, found it. He had heard strange noises and voices. He said he was stuck there for an hour and couldn't find the way out. Something, or someone, always changed the way. This is all very mysterious and I don't like it," said the neighbor Mrs. Bucket as she took a third cookie from the plate. "I'm quite sure it was a ghost. We all know these legends about the ghost caves in the mountains."

"Yes, very strange," replied Idunn's mum as she brought more coffee from the kitchen.

Idunn could hardly suppress her laughter and she hurried to bury her face in her book. Mrs. Bucket loved gossip. She believed every legend and lie she'd ever heard. Idunn was sure there were no ghosts, magic caves or any such things. People invented that nonsense long ago, when they didn't know how the sun moved upon the sky or what caused rain… But in the 21st century we should be smart enough to explain such obvious matters without making up silly magical theories.

***

Days and weeks passed. All the treetops had turned brown and the dried leaves fell one by one, leaving the branches cold and bare. Idunn's mum started a new job that earned much more money, but she was very busy and Idunn saw her only when she returned home, at nine o'clock. Idunn herself was busy too. School finally started and they took tests almost every day. Mrs. Bucket stopped visiting them, but her "foolish stories" were now the main topic of conversation in the village.
"How is your mum doing?" asked Sophie, Idunn's best friend.

"She's doing well," said Idunn, "but she's very busy. Sometimes I feel I'm the only person who lives in our house."

"Aren't you scared?" Sophie asked, "Ghosts like big and lonely houses."

"There is no such thing as ghosts, Sophie! Don't tell me

you believe in them."

"Of course I believe in ghosts." Sophie opened her notebook and began drawing. "Mr. Mason, the new teacher found their cave."

"Don't be ridiculous!"

"I'm not, besides, why would he make that up? But that's not all, he said the only way to get there is across the mountains and you have to follow an old, ugly man with dirty clothes and a walking stick, diamond encrusted."

"Sophie…"

"It's true. The man mustn't see you and you mustn't lose him, otherwise you wouldn't be able to come back."

When Idunn heard such things, she usually said, 'it's just a silly story', but this time she didn't laugh. Something in Sophie's voice told her not to do so. "How do you know all that? Did *you* see him?" She tried to talk in her usual, condescending tone, but she couldn't.

"No, no one except Mr. Mason had ever seen him," said Sophie, "but he is real." The lesson started and they didn't talk about it anymore.

That night, she couldn't sleep. She lay on her back and stared at the ceiling. She was thinking about the old legends she had heard when her mother came to say good night.

"Do you know there is a new rumor, about a man, who shows you the way to the cave?" asked Idunn.

"Yes".

"Why do people tell such stories?" Mum smiled and caressed Idunn's hair. "Because people need supernatural things and heroes, or monsters. Nature has a few rules, but you can't change them."

"Do you believe in ghosts?"

"No."

Idunn smiled. "I'm glad, I'm not the only normal person."

"Did Haylde call?" asked mum, changing the subject. "I wrote her a letter."

"No, I am starting to miss her."

"Good night."

Idunn tried to sleep, but new questions disturbed her. *Where is Haylde? Why didn't she call?*

Haylde was a very good friend of mum. They were the

same age, had a lot in common and used to see each other almost every day. They even worked together for a while, but then Haylde went to the mountains. She was a geologist. Now Haylde lived there, in the mountains, and called mum every month. But now two months had passed and Haylde didn't call.

Idunn knew Haylde, too. She had seen her many times and she really liked this tall, jolly woman with blond hair and big, gray eyes. Idunn sat in bed. *Haylde hasn't called since people started to talk about the ghost cave. Was she related to all this?* Idunn shook her head. *No, there is no such thing as ghosts!*

***

When Idunn woke up it was raining. She got up, put on her clothes and went downstairs to have some breakfast. Mum was at home and had made pancakes. They ate them with maple syrup.

"Aren't you working today?" asked Idunn, licking the sticky syrup on her lips.

"I will go later." said mum. Idunn brushed her teeth, grabbed her schoolbag and put on her shoes. "Goodbye, mum!" she said and went out.

It stopped raining. The wind was nice and the sun was shining. Idunn walked slowly and enjoyed the weather. She wasn't in a hurry. School started at eight o'clock so she had almost an hour to herself. After a few minutes had passed she realized, that she was looking at the mountains.

"What am I doing? " She asked herself and tried to concentrate on the way. But, again, she found herself staring at the distant peaks. She stopped walking and tried to understand why she felt so drawn to them.
There was nothing to see.

Idunn went to the edge of the village, where the rocky walls were very close, three or four meters. Big gray rocks lay randomly on the ground, supported by the closest hills, and gravel covered most of the road and pathways. As Idunn looked up to the high mountaintops, she saw pure, white snow glittering in the sun. There was nothing unusual. Now she needed to go to school. But something didn't let her and she stood there, looking at a narrow stony pathway. It was winding, some places were hidden behind boulders, or other mountains, but then appeared again and went on, until it was too far to see further. Idunn tried to go back, but her legs didn't obey her.

Suddenly, she stopped, frozen with terror.

A little figure was climbing up the pathway. Its back was turned to her, but she could see it was a very old man. His clothes were old and dirty. He had white, slick, long hair and a bent back. But when she looked closely, she saw he was holding a diamond encrusted walking stick in his wrinkled hand.

Idunn was frightened. She wanted to scream and run back as fast as she could, but she couldn't move. As she looked at the old man, she suddenly realized that she was walking after him. Her legs moved very slowly, forced by an unknown power. Her hands were trembling. The fear was unbearable.

It's just a bad dream, she thought, but she knew it wasn't. She had to get out of there. Idunn used all her willpower against the Dark magic controlling her. It was very strong. She had already gotten to the pathway. She felt cold sweat on her forehead and hands. She was trembling but with some effort she stopped walking.

The Dark magic was still there, trying to take hold of her, but she was starting to overcome it. Slowly, very slowly, she turned back and walked to the village. She made her way against the Dark magic as if swimming against the current. Every step was easier and quicker. "I need to get out of here," She repeated to herself. When she was almost running, the Dark magic disappeared. Idunn fell on her hands, got up and ran as quickly as she could back home, leaving her schoolbag on the ground and frightened as never before.

She didn't see anything and almost didn't hear her own heart, beating like a drum, but somehow she could feel, there was no one. The village was empty.

At last, she arrived home, totally exhausted. She got in and locked the door behind her. Mum was still there. "What is it, Idunn, what happened?" she cried and ran to her daughter. Idunn didn't know what to do. She was tired and frightened. Mum said something, but this time Idunn didn't hear her. She fell on the cold floor.

***

Idunn woke up on the sofa in the living room. Mum was sitting next to her, extremely worried.

"What happened?" she asked, "What made you burst into the house like that? Why aren't you at school?" Idunn looked out of the window. It seemed so long ago, even though she could still feel the fear inside herself. But now she was safe, and she was very tired. "I saw him," she mumbled. "Saw who?" mum almost shouted.

"The man from the mountains." whispered Idunn and closed her eyes. She was still trembling, but she fell asleep.

When she woke up again, she was lying on the sofa, but mum wasn't there. The sun was shining through the window and the birds were singing. The sky was light blue, washed clean by the rain. Idunn sat up. She pushed the hair from her face and looked around the room. Everything seemed to be all right. She got up – and fell on the floor. Only now she noticed that she was very hungry. She stood up again and went to the kitchen.

She took an apple and looked at her watch. It was eleven o'clock. "I must have been sleeping for a long time," she thought. "Idunn!" cried mum, who just entered the big room. "Are you all right? I should have been working, but I didn't want to leave you alone… Are you hungry?" she added when she noticed how quickly this little girl was eating. Idunn just nodded, taking another bite.

Mum stood there for a while, clearly concerned about Idunn, and then she cooked rice. Idunn sat at the table and mum sat next to her. "OK," she said, "Now you're going to tell me what happened. What man did you see?"

"I told you," said Idunn, "the man from the mountains."

"What man!?"

Idunn sighed, "This man from the stories, who shows you the way to the ghost – cave."

Mum laughed nervously. "Idunn, there is no such thing."

"That's what I thought too."

There was silence for a moment. "What did he look like?" asked mum quietly.

"Just like Sophie described him. Ugly, bent back, sticky hair, dirty clothes… and a diamond encrusted walking stick." She shivered at the memory of the mountain pathway. Mum didn't say anything and waited for more details. She seemed to believe Idunn, but she still wasn't sure, if it's possible.

Idunn put the half – eaten apple on the table. "I didn't see his face," she said slowly, "but something forced me to go after him. It was so strong… Hadn't I eaten a sweet breakfast I would probably be in the cave by now." She smiled in a sort of dark humor. "I was so weak and so frightened…" Mum didn't answer for a long time. She turned off the stove, put some rice and chicken from yesterday on a plate and gave it to Idunn. She thanked her and started to eat with a spoon. Mum ate only rice, she wasn't hungry.

"I have to go," said mum at last, "but I think it will be better if you stay home." Idunn nodded.

Mum went to work and then Idunn washed the dishes. She took her apple and went upstairs to her room. Idunn lay on her bed. She had a lot of things to think about. *What will Sophie say about all that?*

"I told you – there are ghosts."

No, she couldn't tell anyone about the man. She was annoyed because of the fact that she was wrong, and she was scared too. Idunn put the apple on the bedside table and closed her eyes. She would stay home and forget all this…

When mum came back home, she found Idunn sleeping in her clothes. She didn't wake her up.

Idunn woke up at nine o'clock. Mum had already gone to work. She got up and realized, she was in her jeans. *Great.* The apple was still on the bedside table. Its flesh was brown. Disgusted, Idunn threw it to the bin. Then she stood there and looked doubtfully at the apple. Yesterday the apple was yellow but now the skin looked almost golden. Idunn never saw such a thing before.

She shrugged and went to the bathroom. *It's just an apple, isn't it?*

She brushed her teeth and changed her clothes. Then she checked the house and closed all the open windows. Everything was all right, but she was still afraid. The big house seemed scary when she was alone.

She went to the big cellar. Its floor was made of white ceramic tiles, same as the whole house and it was a light room, although there weren't any windows. It was a large, almost empty space, divided by a wall from the little bathroom originally designed for guests. Idunn sat on the gray sofa beside the wall. A little coffee table stood next to it, holding a very old telephone. It still worked and mum used it sometimes, when she didn't want Idunn to hear her. Idunn looked at it for a while, lost in her thoughts. She jumped from her seat when a noise disturbed her.

The telephone was ringing. She raised the receiver, surprised. "Hello?"

"Hello? Alma?" said a familiar voice from the telephone.

"Haylde!" cried Idunn, "why didn't you call so long?"

"I was busy…Is that you, Alma?"

"What? Oh, no, it's Idunn."

"Idunn! How are you?"

"Fine." She smiled.

"Can I talk to your mum?"

"No, she's not home." Idunn played with the telephone cable between her fingers.

"I forgot, you probably live in another time zone… What's the time in your village?"

Idunn looked at her watch. "It's ten o'clock."

"Aren't you at school?"

"No."

"Are you sick?" Idunn didn't know what to say. She didn't want to lie, but she couldn't tell Haylde the truth. "Kind of."

"Good," she laughed, "so you didn't see the man from the mountains, or something like that, huh?" Idunn felt shivers down her spine. How could Haylde know? She was dizzy.

"Idunn?"

She forced a short laugh. "No, there's no such thing."

The telephone trembled from Haylde's loud laugh. "You're just the same as before." Idunn tried to laugh again, but she didn't really listen to Haylde. *How could she know?*

She didn't have time to think about it because Haylde changed the subject. She asked about school and mum and her work and their new house, they talked for an entire hour.

"I have to go," said Idunn at last.

"Me too."

"OK, bye!"

"Wait! One more thing."

"What is it?"

There was silence for a moment, "I need your help, Idunn."

Idunn laughed nervously, "my help?"

"Yes, you're the only one, who can help us."

"I can't do anything mum or you can't."

"Where are you?"

"At the cellar."

"Do you have a mirror?"

Idunn went to the little bathroom with the phone in her hands, the cable creeping after her. "Yes," There was a mirror on the wall. "I want you to look at yourself," said Haylde. Idunn did so. "Can't you see anything special?"

Idunn looked closely at her reflection. She looked as usual. There was nothing special about her wavy light – brown hair, thin figure and round face. She wasn't very beautiful, but she was quite content with her look. The only special thing was her eyes. One was green and the second was yellow, but she was born like this. "No," she said, "I'm not special at all."

Haylde sighed. "Will you stay home tomorrow?"

"Yes."

"All right, I'll call you the same time. But don't tell Alma anything about this phone call."

"Why? How can I help, Haylde? What…"

There was no time for questions, Haylde hang up. Idunn returned to the sofa and put the telephone back on the coffee table. *Why can't I tell mum?* It was just a phone call. Well, not just a phone call. Haylde knew something about the man from the mountains. And she asked Idunn for help, but didn't say what. Then there was another strange thing.;

'You're the only one who can help us,' that's what she said. *But who was 'us'?*

Idunn left the unraveled cable on the floor and ran to her room. She locked the door after her. Haylde was surely related to this. It was getting more and more weird. *What will happen next?* She thought. Idunn closed her eyes. She was lying on her bed, in her own room, in her house. All the windows were closed, the house was locked.

But she wasn't safe.

The next day she got up at half past nine. She was a bit nervous, but something told her she must go there. She sat on the sofa again, but this time a bit frightened. She had a feeling the room itself was watching her, that she was not alone.

The telephone started to ring.

Idunn raised it quickly, "Hello, it's Idunn," she said, hoping to suppress this horrible feeling by talking. "Hi!" said Haylde, "are you at the cellar again?"

"Yes."

"OK, I'll call you every day and you'll always take it here, all right?"

"All right… but how can I help you? Help who? Why me? I…"

"I know you have a lot of questions, Idunn, but we have to start. You will find everything out in the right time." Idunn didn't answer. She was confused. *Start what?* "First," said Haylde, "you need to sit somewhere. Are there any chairs?"

"There's a sofa," murmured Idunn.

"Great! Is your cellar big?"

"Yes."

"And clean?"

"Yes."

"Is there any other furniture?"

"Just a little coffee table and the telephone."

"Well, this is a perfect place."

Idunn had no idea what the geologist wanted from her, but she did everything she was asked to do. First, she moved the sofa to the center of the big room, but the telephone cable didn't reach it, so she had to find another cable in the little bathroom. That one was short too, so she had to cut the rubber around the wires and connect them without hurting herself or breaking the line.

When she finished, it was almost eleven o'clock.

"Thank you Idunn, I'll call you again tomorrow."

"Why can't I tell mum? She will ask me what I am doing to the telephone."

"Don't worry, she will not go to the cellar."

"How can you know?"

Haylde ignored that question. "Can you do one last thing today, Idunn? Ask Alma to buy five kilos of apples."

"Five kilos?!"

"Yes, we'll need them. Bye!"

"Mmmmhmmm." Idunn went to the kitchen. She had to eat something.

That was a very strange phone call, she thought. *What will Haylde want tomorrow? How can I help someone by moving a sofa and buying apples? Who am I even helping?*

At last she did ask her mum to buy apples. "Why do you need so many apples? Can't you just eat one a day?" "Just like that… because… I can't stop eating them." Of course it wasn't true.

So they bought the apples and Idunn took all of them down to the cellar.

The following morning looked very much like the ones before. Idunn was sitting on the sofa, scared a bit, when the telephone started to ring. She raised the receiver with trembling hands.

"Hello, Haylde!"

"Hello Idunn," said Haylde, "are you better?"

"Ehm… yes." Something told her that Haylde knew she wasn't sick.

"Do you have a cold?"

Idunn didn't know why she said what she said, but she said it, and she couldn't take her words back. "Haylde, there's something I have to tell you,"

"Tell me." Haylde's voice was strangely quiet.

"I… I'm not really sick. When I walked to school last time I saw… I saw…"

"The man from the mountains." So she did know. "Yes."

"Alma is right," said Haylde, "you shouldn't go out. It's getting very dangerous." Idunn didn't answer. "Idunn, are you sure you're not special?"

"Well, my eyes are special."

"That's right. And it's you, not anyone else. You aren't the same as Alma, or me, or your friends. Everyone is different, I mean, everyone is special." As Idunn listened to her, she forgot her fear. She really was special and that made her stronger than any rumor. The only question was how to get over the fear. "I'm telling you all this," she added, "because you can do a little more than other people."

"What do you mean?" Haylde laughed. Her laugh made Idunn feel safe.

"Did you buy the apples?"

"Yes."

"Then take one and eat it." Idunn did so. Haylde continued.

"Now tell me, what happens to the apple flesh, when you leave it half – eaten?"

"It turns brown."

"Right. When did you eat an apple the last time?"

"The day before yesterday."

"And what happened to it when you stopped eating?"

"The flesh turned brown."

"Is that everything?"

"Well, the skin turned almost brown too. It was really golden – colored. I've never seen such a thing before."

"Yes. It can happen only to you. In time you'll see why."

Idunn ate almost half the apple. "What do I have to do with that?"

"You'll have to turn apples gold by touching them. Now stop eating." Idunn stopped.

"Is it brown yet?"

"Not yet…" After a short time the apple started to change color. As the flesh turned brown, so did the skin. But the skin was shining. "It's golden! It's golden!" cried Idunn.

"That is exactly what I wanted you to do. I think it's enough for today. I'll call you tomorrow!"

"Hang on, tell me something about yourself. Mum'll be glad to hear some news. "

"Like what?"

Idunn paused, "I don't know… how's the weather up there?"

"The weather?"

"Yes, here it's not very nice. It rains too often."

"The weather is… OK, I guess… well, I hope you enjoyed your little apple experiment."

"I did," she smiled.

"Bye, Idunn."

"Bye!"

She stayed on the sofa for a while and watched the changing colors of the apple.

"Well that is cool!" she said to herself with a smile. But she still didn't understand how that could help Haylde or Idunn herself. She was sorry she couldn't tell her mum about the call, she was determined to tell her as much as possible if Haylde agreed, although she seemed reluctant to talk even about the weather.

"I'll find everything out. Sooner or later I will."

Haylde did call every day and Idunn didn't stop eating apples. At first she felt a little dizzy, when she turned the apple gold, but then it stopped and she could do it more easily and quicker. The skin changed color by the first bite. She didn't only eat apples.

Haylde told her a lot of other things, not just about cultural foods, but mostly about Norse mythology, which was completely unknown to her. Idunn learned the runes and their meaning, and heard stories about the Tree of Life, the wolves that make the sun and moon move and about the nine worlds.

Haylde told her especially about the gods, like Odin, Thor, Tyr, Loki, Bragi and more. There was one goddess called Idunn. Idunn owned the apples of youth. All the gods had to eat them, otherwise they would get old, or ill. She also was very surprised to hear that, unlike in other cultures, Norse mythology had no ghosts, at least not the way she knew. The creatures most similar to ghosts were Draugrs, so called the undead, which lived in their graves, didn't have any special powers, and had in general a lot common with people, including the fact they were mortal. For some reason, Idunn was glad ghosts weren't mentioned during those long conversations that fascinated her and made her take her mind off the recent events.

She didn't go to school for three weeks. After only a week she almost forgot about the man from the mountains, that now seemed to be nothing more than a bad dream, and everything was all right again, but she knew this feeling wouldn't last long. She had to go to school and find out Haylde' s secret, but she was too scared to leave the house because she was sure she'd see the man from the mountains again. Mum planned to use her vacation days and give Idunn company, but somehow she never had an opportunity. As she felt bad for leaving her daughter alone she once asked Mrs. Bucket to come and visit while she was working. Mrs. Bucket showed up the minute Idunn finished her call. She already heard the neighbor's heavy steps on the stairs and she rushed out of the room to stop her.

"Are you allowed to eat in the cellar, darling?" was Mrs. Bucket's reaction. Only then Idunn noticed she was still holding the half eaten apple in her hand. It was already starting to change color. She hurried to dive into an engaging conversation with Mrs. Bucket and throw the apple away as soon as she could.

However, she couldn't disappear from school without anyone inquiring what she was doing. After the first five days her teacher called. Mum uttered something about Idunn not feeling well, which allowed her to stay at home, but at the end of the week they got another call. Idunn herself was surprised when her mum rejected sending her to school for the second time. By the end of the second week a teacher came personally to see what was going on. It was Mr. Mason, the biology teacher. Idunn invited him to come in, although he was the very last person she wanted to see that moment. She would have left him with her mum, but it was early in the afternoon and she was home alone.

"You look quite healthy, Idunn, I'm glad you're feeling better," he said as they sat in the living room. Idunn just forced a smile. "When will you return to school?"

"I... I don't know. It really depends, I..." to her big surprise he suddenly leaned forward with a keen expression in his eyes. "It's OK, Idunn, I know what you're going through." She stared at him for a moment. "I'm sorry?"

"I myself needed some time to recover, I didn't believe in those rumors either and it was hard for me when they proved to be true…"

With confusion and terror Idunn watched him as he gave her homework for the last two weeks and a permission to stay at home longer. She was too puzzled to say anything and when he left the bad feeling grew only worse. *What does he know? How does he know?*

She immediately grabbed her iPhone and called Sophie. "Hi Idunn, it's been such a long time! Where are you? When will you come back to school? Why…"

"I don't know, I'm still sick. Tell me, Sophie, are you talking about me at school?" At first she tried to sound ill by coughing and pausing, but her curiosity won and she hurried to finish the sentence.

"Everyone's talking about you! They say you stay at home because you hate those rumors and you're too scared to admit they're true. But I know it's not the reason, I know you wouldn't do that…"

"Sophie," she interrupted her, "what do they say about me?"

"Exactly what I just told you, I told them you're not that kind of person, you would at least laugh at them and-" Idunn forced a sudden cough to stop Sophie's prolonged explanations. "I have to go, bye!"

She didn't wait for the answer and hang up. Now everyone was gossiping about her! Idunn didn't like that at all. The little desire she had to get back to her normal life abandoned her entirely. How could that happen? Was she arousing too much attention? Or was it Mrs. Bucket who came up with these lies? The moment those thoughts entered her head she regretted them, she knew Mrs. Bucket was not to blame. Idunn decided to tell Haylde, perhaps she would know what to do, but no one answered her call.

It was hard for her to keep their calls secret. Sometimes she almost revealed everything but then decided it was not the right time and hurried to change the subject. Her indecision grew only worse, mostly because she could see mum missed Haylde. Sometimes she found her looking at old pictures of herself and Haylde together from the time Haylde still lived in the village. Some nights mum would come to Idunn and talk, mostly about her old friend. She tried to call her a few times unsuccessfully and Idunn knew she was sad, even though mum never said so.

Her third week at home was almost over when she went downstairs as usual and leaned to take an apple from the plate. It turned gold by the first touch. Idunn left it on the plate, amazed. She did it!

At this moment the telephone started to ring.

"Haylde, I did it, I did it!"

"Idunn, calm down! What are you talking about?"

"I turned the apple gold by one touch!" Haylde was quiet for a moment. "I knew you can do it," she said at last, "congratulations, Idunn!" Idunn laughed.

"Now you can do all I wanted you to do. I think it's time for you to know why I told you all this."

"Oh yes, tell me."

"Not now, I cannot tell you over the phone."

"Will you finally come for a visit?"

"No. Come to the mountain pathway tomorrow, I'll be there." Idunn couldn't believe this was happening to her. "You mean the place where I saw the man from the mountains?"

"Yes."

"What will mum say?!"

"Idunn, don't tell Alma. Not yet. I'll be there with you, it's all right." Idunn felt shivers down her spine. "OK," she said at last.

"Then I will see you there at ten o'clock, all right?"

"OK," repeated Idunn and hang up.

The man from the mountains isn't there now, she said to herself. *It was a long time ago. And I'll be with Haylde.*

Than why was she so scared? That night Idunn couldn't sleep. The thoughts about the Ghost cave didn't let her. She was awake when mum came to say good night. "Idunn," she said, "can you go to school tomorrow? I think you've been at home long enough. What do you think?"

"No. No, I want to stay here tomorrow."

"Your teacher called me again and asked when you're going back." Idunn covered herself with the blanket. "I'm still afraid to go outside."

Mum sighed, "I know, but you have to get over it."

"Give me two last days and then I'll go to school."

"OK then. Good night." Idunn sighed too. *What am I doing?* She thought just before she fell asleep.

***

"It's ten o'clock. It's ten o'clock, where is she?" said Idunn as she walked from side to side in front of the mountain pathway. She was talking to herself, an automatic response to forget her fear, but it didn't really work. "It's ten o'clock and one minute, that's enough, I'm going home!" She turned back and made her way towards her house, threw another glance at the school's direction, but decided she wasn't in the spirit to deal with her newly earned rumors. She continued walking.

"Idunn!" cried a voice behind her. Idunn turned around. It was Haylde. Idunn ran to her and hugged her. The tall woman laughed. "So you decided to go home?"

"You have no idea how scared I am. What is going on?"

"Don't worry, I'll tell you everything. But let's not talk outside."

"Yes! Right. Want to come to our house?" said Idunn and took a few quick steps to the village.

"Actually, I wanted to go to my place."

"As you wish. Just let's get out of here."

"Then come on! This way." said Haylde and went up the pathway.

"What?" cried Idunn, "I'm not going there!"

"Come on. We don't have time to lose."

Idunn didn't move, her green – yellow eyes wide opened. Haylde went back and looked at her thoughtfully. "It's all right, I'm here with you," she said while offering Idunn her hand.

Idunn grabbed it and they went slowly up the mountain.

"You know," said Haylde, "people always told stories about ghosts and monsters. They just need supernatural creatures. Most of the times there is a supernatural hero too, because all these creatures are on the bad side. I wonder why."

She waited for a while, but Idunn didn't answer, so she continued. "For example, ghosts are known as spirits of dead people. All these people weren't bad, then why are the ghosts bad? I like that there's no such stuff in the mythology I told you about. It makes much more sense, don't you think? There's nothing wrong with death. It happens to all living creatures. People made it supernatural, just because they were scared of it. In fact, this is the only thing we can be afraid of. Death, getting hurt, death of loved ones… But we still don't get how it's important. Living forever is much worse than the fact that you will die one day, if you understand what I mean."

Idunn nodded. It made sense.

"Just very old people understand it. They've seen too

many winters and they understand that everything is the same. Nature never changes, people never change. Only when you get it you're not afraid to die."

"Nothing is changing, but it's never the same. No two snowflakes are alike. Every winter looks a bit different. Everyone is special, just as you said before."

"True, of course," Haylde agreed, "but when you are older, you stop looking at the details."

Idunn wanted to answer, but Haylde shook her head. "Not a word. Don't make noise. Trust me." she whispered and went on. Idunn stayed behind her. The terror overwhelmed her.

It was the man from the mountains.

And this time she let the Dark magic move her legs and control her body.

They walked for a long time. The man didn't turn back. He didn't see them. The only noise was his walking stick knocking on the white stones.

And then he vanished. Disappeared.

Idunn found herself at the entrance to a dark cave. She couldn't feel her legs and she was half dreaming. Haylde was still there and she was unusually pale. "Are you all right, Idunn?" she asked.

Idunn nodded. "Now tell me what is going on."

"You are special. You are young. You can turn apples gold. You are the only one who can help us."

"Help who?"

"The ghosts."

A little blue light slowly appeared from the darkness. The entrance slowly disappeared into darkness. "The golden apples are the apples of youth," said the echo of Haylde's voice, "the ghosts are lost between life and death. Only the apples can heal us… or kill us."

Haylde was blurring. Idunn could see the dark cave wall through her. She didn't believe her eyes and just stood helplessly, asking herself if it was truly Haylde she was looking at or only her own imagination.

There is no such thing as ghosts, she screamed in her mind.

"Oh, there is."

The blue light was growing bigger and bigger. Now there was no way out, and blurry figures began appearing from the pale light. They flew through Idunn and made a circle around her. Their feet were a few steps above the ground.

There is no such thing as ghosts.

She could hear the sound of the wind, blowing, crying, somewhere outside. The figures flew around her, without shape, without voice.

There is no such thing as ghosts.

All the figures closed their eyes. At least the eye - shaped holes in their pale heads. The wind was blowing soundlessly.

There is no such thing as ghosts.

Suddenly Idunn lost track of everything around her, she didn't see anything, she didn't hear anything. When her senses came back to her she saw a little cottage at the top of a mountain. The inside was full of shelves that held all kinds of stones and old books. There was a photo of Idunn's mum, Alma, and Haylde too. The only wall without shelves hosted a little kitchen and a bed. *Is this a dream?* She asked herself, *or am I hallucinating?* After a while it occurred to her that it wasn't anything of the kind. Haylde was using Idunn's own eyes to tell her what happened. Idunn stared at the bed, all of the sudden she knew that Haylde had been lying in this bed for two months. She didn't know if she would die or recover. She couldn't call Alma. One day she woke up in the cave. Dead. Alive. It didn't matter.

There is no such thing as ghosts.

"It happened to everyone here," said the echo of Haylde's voice as the vision faded and Idunn found herself in the cave again, "it's a spell. We don't know where it came from. The spell will cease to exist only if all the ghosts get well or die, just like things have to be. And you, Idunn, can give us the apples."

There is no such thing as ghosts…

"People always say we are bad, but in fact they are the bad ones. We needed their help all this time, they could find a way to break the spell, but they didn't want to."

There is… no such thing… as ghosts.

"That's why we need you, Idunn. You never said we're bad. You never said we exist. You can help us. You see things the way they have to be."

There... is... no... such... thing... as... ghosts.

"It is your choice. Do you want to help us?" Idunn didn't dare to look at the figures directly. There was no doubt. There were ghosts. She knew she had been lying to herself all the time. The hardest thing to do was to believe, and overcome her fear. She had to do it now, or never.

Idunn raised her head. The figures watched her in silence.

"I will help you." she said. The ghosts smiled to her. It wasn't a real smile, not on their unseen faces, but Idunn could feel it somewhere inside, their joy reached her heart and filled it with their thanks. Idunn raised her hand. A red apple appeared in front of her. Her hand trembled. Was this a good idea? What would happen to her if she helped them? Would they disappear? Would she find the way out of the cave? What if the cave disappeared forever?

Her hand was now very close to the red fruit. Now she began to understand why Haylde told her about Norse mythology, mythology without ghosts. She wanted her to become Idunn, to make them mortal, to help them. Idunn took a deep breath. *Nature never changes, people never change. Only when you understand this you're not afraid to die.* The ghosts did understand. It's better to risk your life to save many people, than go on like the others and leave the ghosts half – dead forever. She touched the apple.

She didn't really know what happened next, but all the ghosts mobbed the apple. The golden apple vanished inside the foggy crowd. The cave was lit by blue light and dark shadows danced on the rough walls. There was a sudden scream and everything faded into darkness…

The next thing she knew, she was standing on top of a mountain. Lots of people were standing around her and she heard their thanks again and again. She didn't answer. A few people were lying on the soft grass at the edge of the mountain top. Idunn left the people surrounding her and went to the lying ones. They were dead. It was the first time she saw a dead person, but she wasn't disgusted, or scared. She knew they weren't scared of death and now they could rest. Just like the way it was long ago. One person was sitting. It was Haylde. Idunn sat next to her. Haylde smiled. Her cheeks were now bright pink.

"Thank you very much," she said, "I'm sorry we scared you like that, but it was the only way. If you'll go to the others I'm sure they will be glad to fulfill all your wishes."

"What about you?" asked Idunn.

"Could you do one last thing for me? Tell Alma that I really missed her and everything is all right now."

"I will."

Haylde smiled one last time. Idunn could see she was very tired, but happy. Haylde closed her eyes. She let herself lie on the grass and fall asleep forever. Idunn looked at the tall, jolly woman that she and her mum liked so much and felt the tears roll down her face. But she wasn't sad, or scared. She would never be scared again.

***

Mum and Idunn were sitting on the ground under an old tree. Idunn had just finished her story for the second time and mum stared thoughtfully at the horizon. The first time Idunn told her, mum refused to believe a word, when she finally accepted it she locked herself in her bedroom, crying over Haylde's death. For a few days she was melancholy and quiet. Now she simply said: "I am really sorry I couldn't see Haylde before she said goodbye. Life is not the same without her."

Idunn nodded. "She missed you too, but she was happy. And I'm glad it's all over."

"Me too," a slight smile appeared on mum's face, "I'm proud of you." Idunn smiled.

"But don't you ever do it again!" she added. "I thought we have to take a little break of work and… your apples. Your vacation starts in two days anyway. I want to buy a ticket and fly to the other side, see the world, if you're not afraid, of course."

"That would be great!" cried Idunn. Mum stood up and went home to buy the tickets. Idunn watched the birds as they flew to the other side, above the sunset. What can one be afraid of? Death, getting hurt, death of loved ones… Now Idunn knew that death was a normal part of life and she could live with that, because she was special and that made her stronger than the fear itself. She looked at the basket beside her. Inside there was her power, her hope and her weapon. Golden apples.

A Good Snowy Winter

A GOOD SNOWY WINTER

For my sister,

A bright dot of light in the dark,

The burning torch inspiring me to go on.

At last he realized what had made him so uneasy. The weather. He felt uncomfortable from the very moment he woke up and couldn't find any reason for it. First of all, it was hard to breathe. As if there was an unseen chain around his chest, not letting it soak enough air in. As if it was trying to stop his heart, as if it was saying : *rest for a while, why are you beating without a break?* The voice didn't know that the heart mustn't be stopped, that it had to alert the whole body and pour energy into the mind. The voice was still and wanted the heart to be still too.

"It mustn't be still," he said, mostly to himself because the voice was heard only by him, "I want to think now. And then I'd want to get up and do many other things."

'It is easier to think when everything is still and the mind is resting.'

"Not actually," he said after a short while, "this is what many people think, but it's not true. We would have nothing to think about."

'How could you know? Have you ever tried it? Even when everything looks dead and forgotten it is full of small lives and action. But if you hush and your heart stops nothing would disturb you.'

"We can be calm only when we know that everything is full of life and action…" He sat up with difficulty. "Action, that's what I need."

He closed the window to oust the gray sky from his sight and get rid of the still voice and limped downstairs. It was very cold, as cold as winter should be, but not even one snowflake fell. "Things that look dead are full of action…" he murmured. He continued wondering while cleaning the kitchen table and putting things back to their places because the house was one big mess. George never cleaned anything. George was now sitting careless in the living room.

"Lio?"

"What?" The bad weather had made him anxious too and he definitely didn't have the right spirit for a talk.

"Can you come here?"

"No." He sat down to the half tidied table and sliced a loaf of bread. The chain around his chest tightened.

"Lio?" This time George came to him, took one slice from his plate and watched him with a full mouth.

"What do you want?"

"I want you to look at the old album with me."

"Can't you bring it here?"

"No, it would get dirty,"

Lio smiled, "suddenly you're so clean and careful, huh?" George just continued chewing.

At last he left his untouched breakfast and followed the boy to the living room. A big heavy book was lying on the window seat. The family album. Lio knew a day wouldn't pass without George looking at it at least once. He himself opened it very rarely. The pictures caused him sad memories. He threw the clothes and papers that covered the sofa to the floor and sat down. There was no use of putting them in their place as long as George was in the house. "Here," the boy pointed at a small picture, "tell me about that day."

The picture showed a sunny afternoon. A few trees stood proudly on the background of the bright blue sky, tall and green. Beneath the trees sat a curly haired woman, playing with a baby on the grass. Their smiles shone with happiness as if there were no troubles ever to come. It was a little window back to the past, frozen and motionless, but still full of life that only these who shared that moment could see.

"It was a week before summer holiday," said Lio, "dad was planning our trip but all mum did was play with you. She said she didn't want to go anywhere, just stay here and enjoy the summer. Maybe she forebode that they won't be able to do this for long. At last dad agreed, asked at work for a vacation and we were all here." He closed his eyes, feeling the beautiful memory once more.

"This is me, right?" George pointed to the baby, over excited.

"Yes, that's you."

"And this is you, right?" George turned the page and

examined another view.

This time it was inside the house that was, unlike now, tidied and organized. A nice fire lit the room and snow flew outside the window. A boy was sitting beside a decorated Christmas tree with a present in his hand. The image was adorned with large chaotic handwriting. *Liort 14.*

"What did you get?" The chain suddenly vanished, the heart beating doubled its speed, the eyes went wet. "Put it away,"

"But you didn't tell anything!"

"Not now, George." He didn't know whether George continued arguing or not, he just went to his room again and locked the door and cried quietly until slumber stopped his tears.

***

Lio woke up to darkness. He remained lying until he understood what had happened. He must have slept all day. Cool moonlight that filled the window through the drawn curtains caught his attention. The moon was almost full and it was the 22nd of December. The moon is usually full at the middle of the month, not at its end.

Things that look dead are full of action.

This must be one of these unnoticed actions, he wondered, *what could it mean?*

The door creaked as it opened and the stairs sighed beneath Lio's feet on his way back downstairs. George was still stretched over the sofa, fast asleep with the open book in his hands. It didn't surprise Lio. He knew George was very disorganized, but never had time to talk with him properly. His shadow fell over the sleeping boy as Lio's silhouette covered the far moon. He watched him for a while; his regular breathing, his carefree face, his small unwashed hands and thought of the past and of what was to come next. He caressed George's dark curls, put the album away and raised the boy to get him to bed. The stairs squeaked horribly loud and the sounds that came from his stomach weren't very quiet either. The boy started talking in his sleep and almost fell from Lio's arms.

At last George was safely in his bed and Lio searched for something to eat. The bread he sliced before was probably used as George's dinner, because the plate was empty and crumbs had accumulated on the floor. Now their pantry contained only a few loafs of bread, one jar of honey, another two of strawberry jam, canned sweet corn, eggs and milk. He decided to save the bread, opened the can and ate from it because he didn't want to wash dishes at night. That reminded him he still had to pay for the water and electricity they had used last month. He would have to make more money tomorrow… And buy a few things, as well as help with the preparations for

Christmas. It was hard to ignore his disappointment. He didn't plan to work that week. Lio sat in the living room, looking thoughtfully at the bare plain outside. Suddenly a smile lit his face and all his troubles were forgotten. He slammed the can down on the coffee table so hard that it almost fell on its side, a used sheet of paper was raised from the ground and rustled as gentle words appeared on it one by one.

Wafted slowly by the breeze,

As clear as bell's chime,

Never feeling heat or freeze,

Accompanied by Luna's shine.

He examined the poem, satisfied. But wasn't it too short? It wouldn't get published if he left it like this. He continued writing, not without reluctance. Lio was a poet. He wrote and published his lines in the newspaper. His payment depended on the number of words, although the length was limited. It was quite a poor job, but Lio knew very well how to save his money. Of course he had tried to get a better job, now that he had to take care of himself and his brother without anyone's help, but it wasn't possible in such a small community. Besides, he was glad to stay home with no need to hurry.

George, on the other hand, was quite ignorant of these problems. He was only eleven, ten years younger than Lio. He went to school as long as it was free and was a little celebrity in his class. One girl even brought him a whole basket of lemons and oranges from her father's farm every winter.

Yes, people were nice to them. An old lady - Miss Rose, as Lio used to call her — took care of the two of them until he was old enough to take hold of their parents' house. All this because their parents were gone. They left the year Lio was fourteen. Now another stanza appeared, slowly and bashfully. The ink seemed to tremble on the paper at Lio's discontent glare.

Over endless waves of ocean,

Crossing dark yet well — known plains,

Passing by fields that can't be seen,

Goes my song, searching home and friends.

It wasn't as good as the first verses, but they could catch a reader's attention. He raised the pen once more to make the poem sound finished.

Goes my song, my song goes on,

And I behind it, to give it my voice.

It's all I hear, my ears are void,

But I am glad, it was my choice.

Originally he wanted the poem to be dark and mysterious, as this sleepless night, but the other stanzas had concealed the power of the first one. Although that didn't really matter, not for the newspaper, at least, people like everything to be simple and explained. He remained in the living room all night. At first he was writing, but stopped as his ideas turned into strange melancholy. Then he just sat, but remembered nothing of what he was thinking about. He watched the pale colors of morning pouring across the dark canvas, changing its shade gently. Colors brushed over the sky by delicate cotton, as if powered by unseen hands of a master painter.

After a short moment the stairs squeaked and little George appeared at the door.

"Good morning!" he yawned clumsily and rubbed his eyes, "I thought you've already decided to take a winter sleep." There was silence until he realized Lio wasn't about to answer. "Will you tell me about the photos today?"

"Today you're going to school, George," said Lio without turning his head.

"What?" cried George, "But you said I didn't have to this week!"

"I've got some work to do."

"But yesterday when you wanted to sleep you didn't,

right?"

"Stop arguing and dress up."

At that point George decided to try another method. "Please, Lio…" He meowed in the sweetest voice he could make and widened his green eyes. "No, Georgie…" Answered Lio in the same irritating voice and got up to throw the empty corn can.

The soft, nice stare disappeared at once. "That's not fair!" he cried and stomped up the stairs.

After a short while, though, they both put on their boots and left the house. George carried Lio's old school bag and Lio a collection of newly written poems. They walked in silence. The loudest noise was made by their steps on the road stones. Sometimes they went off the way to let a car or two pass, but otherwise the bare plain didn't change much. When they saw the school building George slowed. "Oh, no!" cried Lio all of a sudden. "What?" The boy seemed a little startled.

"I forgot to lock the house!" He turned back and ran, "go on without me," he cried to George, "and don't you even think about going somewhere else!"

He could only hope George would obey him because the boy was soon out of his view. Lio burst into the house after five minutes' run all out of breath. The keys were on the kitchen table.

"How could I be such a fool?" he murmured. Lio grabbed the keys, checked that all the windows were closed and left for the second time, this time properly.

His first destination was the publishing house. There were a couple of journalists too. They all waited about half an hour until the editor arrived. He was an elderly man who always wore a long, deep green coat and an old fashioned hat. His accent revealed he was a foreigner. Lio laid his poems in a row on the desk. The man examined them for a while. "These two are good," he raised the mentioned two from the table, "and this one isn't bad, it can be printed tomorrow. We can put that one there too, if you make it shorter."

"And what about the last three?"

"People wouldn't read such things."

"But these are some of my best!"

"Of course, of course," the editor smiled and tried to look as if he had the same opinion, "but people, you know, don't judge the poem according to its poetic devices. Goes my song, who would like to read that?"

"Last week you told me to write more sentimentally." Lio was quite insulted.

"Yes, yes, but without all these metaphors and… and… Metaphors."

Lio sneered, "it's a personification." The man smiled apologetically. Lio sighed. "How much will you give me?"

An hour later he exited the publishing house with his shortened and changed poems and a little heavier wallet. The next stop was the flower shop. He passed by the colorful bouquets, picking up a single red rose. "Are you tired of the pink ones, Liort?" asked the saleswoman. "No, I just thought a change wouldn't be bad," and spent a fifth of his income on the precious flower.

Then he stepped back on the road which led him all the way to a snow – white house. He knocked on the wooden door. A short gray haired woman opened him.

"Hello, Liort!" she said with a smile on her wrinkled, pleasant face and invited him to come in.

Lio gave her the flower. He always brought Miss Rose flowers, and only roses. She accepted it happily and hurried to put it in a vase full of water. "Will you join the Christmas dinner tomorrow?" asked Miss Rose.

"Well…"

"What?" she interrupted him with a glint in her eye, "last year's excuse was George's sickness and the year before you said you had to fix the faucet. What will it be now?"

"Well…" Lio looked around at the large living room they had just entered. Most of the furniture was already moved to the upper floor and six or eight desks were arranged into one long dining table.

Miss Rose made a big Christmas feast every year and invited more than half the village. Lio never joined it. When they still lived with the old Miss he used to spend the entire day before outside without his coat so he would get ill and wouldn't be forced to celebrate. He had kept avoiding the parties when they left the white house too. Sometimes he would send George but he himself never came. "I don't expect you to celebrate, Liort, I know you don't like it," she said kindly, "We all just want you to be with us. Especially on your own birthday." Lio lowered his head. Miss Rose waited for an answer, but then decided it would be better to drop the subject. "Come and set the table, I'll decorate the windows."

After a few hours' work the whole room was decorated with cleaned green and red ribbons, the only furniture were the chairs around the big table that was covered with a white cloth and set with shiny silverwares. A spruce stood near the fireplace and a box full of delicate glass ornaments waiting to be hung. The old lady placed the red flower at the center of the table with a smile. Her smile dwindled when she turned back to Lio. He couldn't smile. He felt truly bad because of their conversation. Miss Rose smiled again, in an attempt to comfort him. "You'd better have lunch with me," she said, "come on." And she led him to the kitchen. There she seated him beside a small table, brought two bowls full of hot soup on it and sat down too. They ate in embarrassing silence.

"I have to go," said Lio at last and got up, leaving his bowl half – full. The old woman glanced at the clock, sighed and nodded. "This is for you," she handed him a bar of milk chocolate, "and this is for George," and gave him another one. Lio smiled, kissed her creased cheek and left. In fact, he had plenty of time before George finished, he just wanted to leave Miss Rose. It happened to him often in many occasions and he was always ashamed of himself, but couldn't help it. Lio was never good at relations with people.

At one o'clock he was standing in front of the school entrance with a small plastic bag which contained a few cans, milk, eggs, a box full of tea bags, and the chocolate from Miss Rose. Lio wandered around the village for half an hour, and at last he decided to wait for George. He didn't want to go home alone. The school bell rang loudly from inside the building and children started pouring out. Lio stood on his tiptoes to try to see his brother. The entire street was suddenly full of children. There were small children who ran to their waiting parents, bigger children, talking and acting stupid in front of the school, and even the oldest students who were almost his age. He was sure the noise in the lane could be heard now throughout all the village. Lio noted that he didn't like the place. His eyes wandered, trying to find the small boy amongst the crowd.

"Hello, Liort," said a quiet voice next to him. He turned

to the speaker. It was a girl of sixteen or seventeen. Her slim figure was wrapped in a heavy coat and her thick hair cascaded down her shoulders. She gazed at him with a small smile. Lio frowned. How did she know him? Have they ever met? Could he have possibly forgotten? "Hello," he uttered. Then a curly haired child at the other side of the street caught his attention. "George," he cried and waved at him to come. When he turned back to the girl she was gone. At that moment he felt a strange aching in his stomach that told him something wasn't right. He moved a few steps and searched all around him to find the girl in the crowd but it seemed she had vanished.

"What are you doing, Lio?" cried George when he reached him.

"Where is she?"

"Who?"

"I don't know," he said, still standing on his tiptoes, searching the crowd helplessly, "one moment she was here and... Then she was gone!"

"Who? Your fairy godmother?"

"Don't be silly!" It was clear George enjoyed this conversation. He smiled gleefully. Lio shook his head angrily. George began to walk away so he gave up his useless efforts and followed him.

"It was so unkind of you to send me to school today," complained George after a few minutes.

"Why? What did you do?"

"Nothing! I'd rather learn!"

"Really? Then it was very good for you," laughed Lio.

George looked away crossly.

Lio didn't try to make him speak. He talked to George only when it was necessary. Maybe life shouldn't be that way, he didn't know. It was too late to change that now. The boy ran upstairs as soon as Lio unlocked the house. "Come and help me tidy the living room," cried Lio after him.

"No,"

Lio put the shopping into the pantry and started putting things in their places alone. When he had half – finished George came back and sat down in front of him, behaving exactly as Lio thought he would. He watched him clean for a while.

"I'm hungry," he declared at last.

"Of course you're hungry," he countered, "you had only a slice of bread for breakfast."

George opened the pantry. "Can I eat the strawberry jam?"

"No,"

"I wouldn't complain if I made me a stomachache,"

"Yes you would."

"But Lio! We've been living on bread for the last three weeks!"

"Because you refuse to eat rice and you refuse to eat potatoes and…"

"OK, I think I won't refuse in the future. I just can't eat bread anymore."

"That's too bad. We have nothing else." So George had bread for lunch.

Lio was quite content with his work. The living room looked cleaner than ever. Of course it wasn't as clean as Miss Rose's, but it wasn't bad. He continued to the kitchen. This time George helped a little. He did very well, except for spilling water all over the floor while washing his plate.

Darkness came soon. The ground floor of the house was respectably organized and the two boys ate their "dinner bread" at the light of the old lamp. When he finished George gave a great yawn, rubbed his green eyes and went to bed without another word. Lio didn't move from his place. He had to write a Christmas poem for tomorrow and bring it early in the morning. It was hard even for such a poet as himself to describe how he disliked to write about predetermined themes. He took out his papers and a pen and looked for a clean page. He stopped browsing when he saw the poem he wrote the night before.

Wafted slowly by the breeze,

As clear as bell's chime,

Never feeling heat or freeze,

Accompanied by Luna's shine.

Over endless waves of ocean,

Crossing dark yet well — known plains,

Passing by fields that can't be seen,

Goes my song, searching home and friends.

Goes my song, my song goes on,

And I behind it, to give it my voice.

It's all I hear, my ears are void,

But I am glad, it was my choice.

"*Goes my song,* who would like to read that?" he whispered with a bitter smile, "Oh, well. It's not that good after all."

***

The next day his alarm clock woke him at 5 a.m. He couldn't conceal the smile that appeared on his face. Lio jumped out of his bed and ran to the window to see if it was snowing.

It wasn't. This unsettled him a little, but then his smile returned. At half past five he met the editor at the publishing house and at six he was back home with a good amount of money. George woke up quite early too, and when he ran down the stairs at a quarter to seven he found two cups of tea, fresh hot pancakes, and two bars of chocolate on the tidied table. He looked at Lio to find out the meaning of this. To his surprise, Lio looked sincerely happy. George almost forgot how that looked expression on his brother's face.

"Merry Christmas," was Lio's explanation. George bit his lips. How could he forget? He ran back to his room and his quick steps could be heard through the ceiling. After a moment he came back with a satisfied smile. "Happy birthday, Lio," he said, giving him a paper bag. Lio opened it. Inside there was a little notebook. "Calendar 2013?" he laughed. George nodded.

"I guess it's the same one you gave me the last four years?" George nodded again. "How do you always get it back?"

"When you're away."

Lio giggled.

"But this time," cried the boy, "I have a real surprise." He waited dramatically, "I found your lost book," and handed him a copy of <u>The Memoirs of Sherlock Holmes</u>. This present was much more successful in impressing Lio. "Thank you, George! Where did you find it?" He uttered half a sentence and focused on his breakfast. He waited until Lio finished his pancake and then ended the silence.

"The weather is very nice today, isn't it?" Lio nodded with a suspicious look. "I'm so glad I can stay home!" he continued. The following ten minutes he talked about the nice atmosphere and of how content he was. "Would you like me to give you half of my chocolate bar, Lio?" He asked at last.

Lio observed him for a while. "You're trying to catch me in a good mood to tell you about the photos, right?" George bit his lips again, giving another nod. Lio's smile vanished. "All right," he murmured at last.

"A month after you were born, we had a mole in the garden. Grandpa came for a visit and decided to get rid of it. It wasn't easy. At first it was only him who tried to catch it. Then dad joined him, then the neighbor, then old Peter…"

George laughed, "There are ten people in this picture."

"Yes."

"I'm sure they didn't catch it at all."

"They did, but they took it to the fields. It came back within a week."

George asked about the image on the other page. "That's me and dad," Lio said.

"What are you doing?"

"I don't know!"

It seemed the boy didn't care about Lio's bad temper

starting up. He skipped a few pages. Now they saw an image as twice as big as the others. It showed a large plain, covered with soft snow. Children of different ages stood there in an uneven row. Some of them were smiling and some were looking in a totally different direction. Some were kneeling down to play with the snow and some were picking their noses. "I remember this!" cried George, "It's the school picture. The kindergarten belonged there too, back then. This is me," he pointed at a four – year – old child that held a snowball in his mittens. "And this is probably you, right?" and pointed at a young teenager at the opposite side of the row. It was clear he hadn't touched the snow, for his winter clothes were clean. He was smiling slightly at the camera exactly as they were all probably asked to do. Lio nodded. "I know it was a good, snowy winter," remarked his brother, "not bald and colorless and depressing like the last few years. There had been less and less snow and this year it isn't snowing at all."

"Yes, it's because of the global warming." They looked at the picture for a while.

"Who is this?" asked George at last while examining one of the bigger girls.

"This is Emily, her family left to the city a year later."

"And this?" He pointed at a girl that looked more like a

woman than the others. She stood so close to the children that their arms touched, but she still looked so different, as if her figure was cut from another photograph and stuck to this one where it didn't belong. It was impossible to overlook her although she didn't look particularly special at all. She wore a long winter coat with her dark thick hair falling over her shoulders. "I…" Lio examined her face, knowing that it was familiar but the reason escaped him, "I don't know."

"Do you remember seeing her at least?"

"I… I don't know."

***

"And finally, I would like to wish you all a happy and successful new year." With this sentence Miss Rose finished her long speech and all the assembled people started talking in an instant. It wasn't quiet when dinner was served either and the noise grew even louder at its end. Children who couldn't sit still were running and playing all over the room, their parents watched them anxiously and all the others talked and laughed loudly. Then some got up, some moved the chairs, and they were soon divided into many small groups, each with a different conversation. All that time Lio sat silently near the farther end of the table. He hardly ate anything and was all stressed out. Sometimes someone would politely ask him a question or two, but otherwise no one disturbed him. He watched George, who was his little orientation spot amongst the people, to have something to do and to feel he wasn't alone in that situation, not that George cared for being there. He immediately became the other children's main attraction and quite enjoyed it. Miss Rose left her guests behind and came to him for a moment. "Are you sure you don't want me to say anything about your birthday?"

"Please don't."

"Won't you come and join us?"

He forced a smile. "Maybe later."

Then she went off again. Lio watched the guests carefully, sometimes glancing at George to comfort himself a little. At last politeness made him get up and talk a little with the others, and had to smile and laugh because of everything they thought to be funny. After an hour or two he thanked Miss Rose, caught George and left. Once outside he took a deep breath and calmed down a bit. George didn't complain and didn't criticize him. He knew that not everyone felt well with company, especially Lio, although he never showed that. "I have some pictures," he said and raised their father's old camera. Lio nodded, glad that he didn't mention the visit itself and they started off. It was nearly eleven when they reached home. George sat by the radiator to warm his frozen fingers. Lio warmed some water for tea and looked at the pictures in the camera. Most of them were unfocused and the others badly taken. They both looked at them until the kettle whistled. Lio turned off the camera.

"Wait!" cried George all of a sudden. He gave him a questionable look.

The boy turned it on again and found the picture that drew his attention. "Look," he pointed at a person in the photographed crowd. It was a young woman with beautiful thick, dark hair. She was modestly dressed, unlike all the others in their best clothes and jewels. She was quite hidden amongst them, but still looked as if she didn't belong in the scene. "That's strange," said Lio, "I didn't see her there. But I have a feeling I've seen her somewhere before." He tried to remember, but in vain. George tried too. Every time Lio thought he remembered, she slipped away again.
"I know!" George cried at last, "she's the girl in the school picture!" He ran to get the album, found the old school photo and examined it carefully. Lio looked over his shoulder. But the girl wasn't there. "She was right here, I swear!" It took Lio a while to remember, but even after that he wasn't quite sure if he had seen her there. How could he see her in a picture where she doesn't appear?

That night Lio couldn't sleep. He turned from side to side trying to rest. The moonlight seemed lighter than ever and the sounds outside so loud that he could count how many crickets jumped in the garden. At last he got up and exited his room still in his pajamas. With the door left open, he crossed the hall to get to the ground floor, but stood still as he reached the stairs. The window in front of the stairs was open. "Strange," Lio thought, "I know I closed it before going to sleep." Did George open it?

Perhaps. He turned his back to it with a shrug. A wide moonbeam crossed the parquet to the stairs which led upwards. That didn't surprise Lio, the full moon shone right through the window behind him. What did surprise him was that the moonbeam continued upstairs where the window light couldn't possibly reach. Lio took a step forward. The floor squeaked. After a worried peek into George's room he continued. The moonbeam led him up and up shining as a silver path until at last he got to the attic. It was a large space between two sloping wooden walls. No one had entered this room for years. It had been used as storage for all kinds of forgotten and broken things, from furniture to pencils and colored inks. A strong smell of molding wood filled the room.

He followed the light one step after another. It led to the part of the room where the ceiling was so close the floor that he had to sit down. The light stopped on a small wooden box. Lio raised it. It was the same box his mother used to keep her letters in. She never let him open it, so he never did and it was forgotten. The light faded slowly. He had to go if he didn't want to stay in total blackness. This time he took the box with him.

***

"I've had the strangest dream," said George.

Lio forced himself to open his eyes. The birds had just started to sing to the rising sun and dim morning light filled his room. For some reason his bed was cold. He sat up to see why. The explanation woke him entirely. "George! What are you doing here?"

"I've had a dream," said George, who had thrown the blanket off and was now sitting on the bed close to Lio's feet.

"That's really nice, but do you consider it as a good reason to wake me up like this?"

"I thought you should know,"

He looked at the clock on the bed side table. It was three a.m.

"Whether if I know it now or four hours later, it doesn't make any difference. So go to bed." And he closed his eyes again.

"I've dreamed you went to the corridor. There you stopped to close the window, but then you started following something and after a while I noticed it was a silver line on the floor."

"That did happen, George, you were just sleepy," he answered in a muffled voice from under the pillow.

"But then how do you explain I could see what you did in the attic?"

Lio sat up again, "did you follow me?"

"No, I was dreaming."

"Fine, what did I do next?"

"You found a map."

"I found mum's letter box, you probably followed me half – asleep and imagined it."

"I didn't!" George jumped down angrily and grabbed the old box. He opened the lid.

"Stop! Mum didn't want us to open it!"

"Mum isn't here anymore, Lio, when will you understand that?"

He could have taken the boy out of his room that moment, he could have told him exactly what he thought of all this business, he could have at least answered, but he was silent. There was really no use in continuing to live the same way they had so long ago, with people that would never return. He had always known that deep in his heart, but he went on. Day after day, year after year. What else could he do? He was never able to face his loss and take it as it was and he never would. He promised to do his best, for himself and for his brother, and he did, he really tried, although his way was always a little sad and gloomy. 'You're almost grown up, Liort,' his father said back then, 'you're ready to take care of George.' But he wasn't.

"Don't cry, Lio," George said, sitting down again.

"I'm sorry, kid," he whispered and wiped the tears.

"Now look," he put the open box in Lio's lap. It was full of handwritten letters, some of them so old that the paper started to mold. His hands trembled as he reached for the letters. It was the first time he didn't obey what he was told, maybe the first time in his entire life. His hands trembled again. He raised the first letter. The small paper it was written on was now yellow because of the bad conditions in the attic. The words were written in a hurry, and he could see that was his father's large handwriting. It read:

'My dear friend, Ellie has now found my bag out. Thanks for your help. The map there was also found and seen untouched. You should rest now. I'll be home. Tell me or her if needed?'

Lio didn't see any reason for writing these lines in such a hurry. It looked like a usual explanation, except for that a bag can't be found out. Maybe the addressed person was ill and needed to know without delay? No, such a small thing couldn't bother anyone that much. Perhaps father had to go somewhere and was late. The next piece of paper was cleaner and the handwriting small and organized. This time it was his mother's.

'George,

Many many thanks for everything. I mean it. Won't you come, tell what's new?

Ellie'

George? Lio glanced at his brother who watched him anxiously. Who is George? And thanks for what? Was it the same person who helped dad find the bag? There was neither an address nor a date on the letter. Oh well, it wasn't that serious, Lio was just used to looking for mysteries in everything. The only question that really did bother him was: who is this George?

Meanwhile, his own brother George waited in silence. It was obvious that he wanted to see the letters too, but waited for Lio to finish. He understood that the whole situation was hard for him. Lio always thought he didn't notice, but he did. George wasn't that childish after all.

Lio took out a third letter,

'Ellie,

Tell Robert it's all right. The book of old Peter, in Mill Street is copied now. Find all there. Sincerely,

George'

What a confusing letter! Lio picked up another one, then the one beneath it. 'Sincerely, George... Thanks, George... Dear George... See you, George... George...' Lio found himself breathing heavily. George, be who it may, must have been a very important person in his parents' life but they never said a word about him. He must have been, if they named their son after him... He emptied the box in a hurry, taking the last letter.

'Leave blue boat at round way once. You can miss my white rose write a will but do take now fire care about second of street see the cat in boys. Rain hard meet me and as like the usual.

George.'

"What..." he whispered and turned the paper over again trying to find a reasonable explanation for this senseless note. After a moment of confusion he noticed that the paper was torn out of a diary. The date was 25th December, 2010. Dizziness overwhelmed him. He lied down again, murmuring the date. "I can't believe it."

"Sincerely, George?" cried his brother who grabbed one of the messages, "What on Earth..."

"I need to get outside,"

The sky was gray and the chilly air pinched him. The frozen grass broke beneath his feet as he ran to the garden. Why did mum keep her letters secret? Why were they so important? He couldn't understand how he had never noticed any of these short notes. Why did he only open that box if he had nothing to do with it? But that name, George… What if he was supposed to find all this out? Maybe there was a message for him in these letters, for him and for George. Lio shivered and went back inside. It was a cold day. He knew he couldn't get any sleep now so he stayed in the living room. George accompanied him after a while. "What do you think?" he asked.

"I don't know."

"Have you ever heard about this George?"

"No,"

George sat down next to him. "I've found this," he showed him a small piece of paper. When Lio examined it carefully he saw it was a primitive map of the village. One building was marked in a circle. The old mill. Again his calmness disappeared. The dream was right! He did find a map in the attic. What was that supposed to mean? He was too tired, too confused to imagine the possibilities. Lio got up. He ignored George's questions and reached for the only thing that could calm him down in such a moment; a book. The smell of paper, the feel of the old pages, the sight of the well-known words. <u>The Memoirs of Sherlock Holmes</u>. He opened the old book to the story called the 'Gloria Scott'. Yes, he knew it would help him. "I have to think it all over, don't interrupt me," he murmured, going up the stairs. At first he sat on the bed, trying to soak in the feeling of the story and nothing else, to disappear. Only when he became more self-confident he opened his eyes to read.

"I have some papers here," said my friend Sherlock Holmes, as we sat one winter's night on either side of the fire, "which I really think, Watson, that it would be worth your while to glance over.

These were the first lines. Lio could hear his father's voice pronouncing the words as if he was sitting by his side. This was his favorite story. These very words had been in his memory, since before he was three years old. His father told him the story again and again like an old memory he liked to share. Sherlock Holmes became a part of the family, this memoir in particular. It was thanks to that Lio first became interested in literature.

These are the documents in the extraordinary case of the Gloria Scott, and this is the message which struck Justice of the Peace Trevor dead with horror when he read it."

A scene from the past entered his memory, the river and

the old mill on a lovely spring day. Lio was sitting with his parents on the grass, listening to Holmes's speech. "Now listen carefully," said dad all of a sudden, "you mustn't let the message strike you. You'll need to know all this one day."

The message ran:

'The supply of game for London is going steadily up. Head keeper Hudson, we believe, has been now told to receive all orders for fly-paper and for preservation of your hen-pheasant's life.'

Lio smiled. How surprised he had been the few first times he heard this. Now he knew exactly what the message said. The game is up. Hudson has told all, fly for your life. It was a simple code. So simple no one could solve it. He laughed. When he was young he used to look for such codes in every text, refusing to understand there wasn't one. Even a nonsensical letter could have an important meaning.

He continued reading.

"You look a little bewildered-'

The book fell to the parquet floor. Lio jumped up. Was it possible that...? No. He walked from one side of the room to the other. His thoughts flew through his head like leaves in a gust. A nonsense letter, the need to know all this one day, a hidden message, his father- Lio grabbed the box. He remembered the strange way the words stood. "Find the bag out, won't you come, tell what's new, find all there, leave blue boat," it all led him to one thing: the <u>Gloria Scott.</u>

"George," he cried, "bring me some paper and a pencil!"

***

"What are you doing?" said George in a somewhat derisive voice, "did Mr. Holmes give you inspiration?" No answer came from Lio. He knelt down and wrote something on the paper.

"Is it because of mum's letters? Tell me, I was the one who opened the box, you know." Lio ignored the questions and reached for another message. "Why are you so tensed? Is there a secret code or something? Like in that book about daVinci?"

Silence. Not that George expected anything else. "Come on, tell me! Please, Lio…" To his surprise Lio's eyes fixed on him for a moment.

"You should get some sleep," he said at last, "you have school today."

"I don't need to go, we won't be learning anything, it's still Christmas time."

"Go to bed…"

George would have continued arguing, but Lio got up and went back to his bed, leaving the papers on the floor as they were. Only then the boy left, not without throwing an angry glance back to his brother. When Lio was sure that George had fallen asleep he got up carefully and collected all the papers. He wasn't certain if he was right or why, but he started to think that the secret messages and his parents' disappearance were a mystery, and for some reason he felt that he was the one who was meant to solve it.

After putting the notes back in the box he dressed up, combed his hair, checked on George, and went out, taking the box with him. It was only when he closed his coat that he realized he had forgotten to brush his teeth. Well, never mind, he could do that later. He had left a message for George to go to school without him.

It was raining slightly. Such weather always stimulated Lio's bad temper. His whole idea seemed suddenly so ridiculous, but he promised himself to try. He soon let himself dive into his thoughts and trusted his legs to take him to the well-known place.

The old mill stood by the river near the edge of the road. How much had time passed since he had last been there was hard to tell. At least six years. He avoided it mostly because it had played a major role in his childhood. Every time the mill happened to enter his memory Lio's spirit lowered, very much the same as with the family album George liked so much. Sometimes it seemed to him that George was lucky. He couldn't remember all the time spent at the mill with their parents. He didn't really remember them. Every year his memory of them became fainter, like a fading dream that never came true. George said it was a curse, Lio told him it was a blessing.

Usually the old mill was a charming place, but that day there wasn't any grass at all, the water was brown with dirt, the remains of the mill cold and uninviting. It wasn't a real mill, not anymore, only the ruins of it. Lio was quite sure it was a clue. Another clue from his parents. It was the place they had visited the most. Also, it appeared in the letters. Lio entered the mill and took out his drafts.

'My Ellie found out. Your map also seen. Should I tell her?'

'George, thanks. I won't tell. Ellie.'

'Ellie, it's the old mill, copied all. George.'

The third letter wasn't the only one mentioning this place. Since the code was originally from Sherlock Holmes, it could be quite possible that the next steps of the mysterious person would be related to the book as well. Lio knew these methods well enough to believe that if this other George had copied something from here it meant that he couldn't have taken it. Lio wanted to find whatever it was.

He expected a statue, or an unusual type of bricks. His mother had always looked at such details when they traveled. He looked around for it but found nothing of the kind. His courage abandoned him for a minute, but he wouldn't give up. Perhaps they couldn't have taken the wanted object, but they could've hidden it. He closed his eyes and thought of all the places his parents had showed him most often. It turned out to be harder than expected. His first guess was the hole in the ground next to the small window which had no glass now. It was empty, except for a few branches and a dead bird. He hurried back to the entrance.

Soon enough it was obvious that there was no part of the mill which his parents had showed him in particular. He felt the familiar chain tightening around his chest. Why was he hoping if he had so small a chance? There was no use in fighting his feelings this time. George will wake up soon, Lio knew he should hurry to arrive home before George found out that Lio had gone out. He turned to leave just when the wall on his right caught his attention. It was right beneath the part of the roof that had collapsed and where the wall itself was thickly overgrown with ivy. Lio always imagined the hedera was made of green gold, and he even thought he could hear it chime faintly in the breeze. He remembered telling it to his mum, and she told him to write it down. She told him the plant was indeed fragile and mustn't be touched. He took a step forward. Mum's words reached him again, *"the ivy is fragile and it mustn't be touched."* This time he didn't listen. He reached the wall. His hand caught the green leaves. He ripped the ivy. A series of medieval paintings appeared in front of him.

***

The house wasn't locked when he arrived. The drops soon turned into a hard rain, he had escaped just in time. It was now past ten, George had apparently left. Lio found the pantry open and one jam jar on the floor, with the jam was spilled everywhere. Lio bit his lips angrily. Of course George couldn't leave the house tidy. He placed the box he was holding next to the album in the living room with a loud sigh, fetched some napkins after wasting his time looking for a cleaning rag, and started to clean the mess. He soon acquiesced to his position. At least the work helped him organize his confused thoughts.

A shadow of fear hung over him. The more he thought of his discovery, the bigger the shadow grew. His parents were involved in a mystery, a real mystery, not like the ones in books. Suddenly the fictional world he loved turned into a real one that did not suit him at all. He was no detective, he had no way to find the end of this tangled case. It was better not to consider the option of the end missing. A flash of anger towards his parents lit within him. Not only had they left with no explanation, not only had he a household and a brother to take care of, but they also just couldn't save him from the trouble they started. A trouble they had introduced in such a complicated way, and so long after they had left. He had no choice but to follow them. The matter was getting serious. Lio knew it was impossible for him to go on alone. He needed someone to aid him; Someone stronger, less emotional, someone who wasn't in the same, horrible position as he. By the time the floor was cleaned up Lio was sure that this John Watson of his would be no other than George himself. He ate his breakfast hastily, grabbed mum's box again, took the wallet, the keys, his phone and George's old phone. They never used them, but it was good to have them within reach.

His steps were unusually loud as he walked through the corridors of the school. He imagined their echo must have doubled the noise he made. The feeling of a student coming late for class returned to him for a while. It happened to him only twice in his career, but the idea of interrupting still seemed to him incorrect. He hushed the feeling, telling himself that he came for his brother and the teachers wouldn't mind. They were proud of him. Some newspaper clippings of his poetry were hanging right at the entrance to show all visitors what good results their education brought. He knocked on the door of George's class. All the children were delighted by his interruption. The old teacher who had absolutely no control over her class wasn't delighted at all when he asked for George. Lio felt his cheeks turn red when he heard the children laughing and crying out loud parts of his poems. He closed the door as soon as George sneaked outside, glad to leave the romping children behind.

"This is a joke, right?" he asked, trying to conceal a smile.

"I never joke, remember?" retorted Lio as he hurried to

get outside.

"Why did you leave so early today?" cried George as he ran to catch Lio. Again he got no answer, so another question followed. "Does it have something to do with mum?" And then another; "where are we going?"

"You'll see."

"Did you see the teacher's look when I left?" laughed George, "you must do it more often!"

After about five minutes of walking in silence, that is, except for George's enthusiastic laughter, Lio handed him his phone. "Just in case you'll get lost," he explained.

"Why? Where are we going?"

"You'll see," repeated Lio as he doubled his speed again.

They reached the mill within five minutes of their quick pace. It was hard for George to keep Lio's speed, so when they arrived he was out of breath and simply followed Lio without asking any questions. Only when they stood beneath the roof of the ruined building Lio took out the deciphered messages. "It's a simple code from the <u>Gloria Scott</u>," he said, "I came here to see what they needed to copy down. I still don't know why and what they were hiding, but I think we can make it out of this," he pointed at the wall that looked so bare without the plants on it.

George's eyes widened. "Is it a comics or something?" he whispered, "why do you think we need to check it out? Did you think mum and dad- Wait, did you try to copy it?" He was holding a wet paper with the stick-men drawings Lio made that morning. Yes, he did try to copy it.

"Let's say I'm not a very good painter."

"That's really ancient, isn't it?" said the boy and came closer to examine the blurred painting.

"It's medieval. From the Middle Ages. That means it was long ago, George."

"Medieval! They still had angels back then, right? That's why they paint them so much."

"They didn't, they were only very religious,"

"I didn't know they had comics back then."

Lio buried his face in his hands. "They didn't!"

George looked back at him. "But this is a comics."

He raised his head. "No, I..." he stopped in the middle of the sentence. When he looked carefully, he saw there were the same characters in each picture. Sometimes even the same background. And every illustration was followed by a text.

"How did you…?"

"Oh, you know," said George, "I'm really clever."

They took the first train to town. For the whole hour of sitting there Lio felt incredibly unsure of what he was doing. After all, if the painting in the mill was just a coincidence, then he had lost much of his money pursuing it, and an entire day of his precious time, which he would never get back. The station was crowded and the noise gave him a headache, so he grabbed George and escaped outside as quickly as possible. Rain started again. Still holding his brother's hand, Lio went on to find their destination.

"It's been so long since we came to town last time," said George and looked excitedly around, "I remember that shop! And that house! And this restaurant over there was still closed back then!"

"Maybe because it was Sunday." Lio couldn't help murmuring. The streets became slippery in the rain and they had to be very careful to keep their balance. Lio's clothes were wet although he was wearing a coat and his hair stuck to his forehead. This uncomfortable situation made him hurry and he fell twice on the hard pavement.

"What exactly are we looking for?" cried George over the thunders of the storm.

"A tiny book shop, with a red door," he said.

"What's it called?"

"Antique books or something like that,"

"Could it be the shop over there?" George asked and pointed on a small green painted door, almost hidden in the space between two large houses. The words Antique Books were written on the glass. He stared at it for a while, then nodded and almost slipped again. They crossed the street and got inside.

They entered a narrow, dim lit room filled with ancient books. The shop seemed rather gloomy in the yellow light of a single old lamp hanging from the wooden ceiling. The warmth inside was a great relief after the freezing weather in the street. They stood rooted to their place for a minute, not knowing what to do. Then, carefully to not wet the books they went to the back part of the narrow store. A wall of books separated it from the rest of the shop. There were a few old chairs and a desk. An old, short, stout man was sitting in one of them, reading a golden-covered book. He closed it when the boys came near and examined them with a critical look.

"What do you want?" he said at last.

"Good afternoon," started Lio formally, "we're looking for a book I've heard you have."

The man grinned. "I have lots of them. Which one?"

"I don't remember the name," continued Lio who tried to ignore the man's bad temper, "it's about medieval wall paintings." The old man mumbled something and got up with some difficulty. He walked to one of the shelves. Lio grabbed George's hand just before he touched one of the old books. "Don't touch anything. Your hands are wet," he whispered.

For the first time since they entered the man looked at George. His eyes widened and the sleepy mist that seemed to hang over him disappeared. "I know your face," he said, "you remind me of... wait, I'll remember..." This confused George so much that he didn't even try to argue with his elder brother. "Why yes! You remind me of Ellie! It's been a long time since I saw that girl."

"She's my mum," replied George after a while.

"Your mum? Well, that shouldn't surprise me. What's your name, kid?"

"George."

A smile appeared on the man's face. This made him look almost nice. "George, huh? And you?" turning to Lio,

"You must be the older one." He nodded. "I remember you, Dragonlord. One can't forget such a name." It took him a while to understand what the man meant. Then he smiled and nodded. "Do you know who I am?" continued the owner of the shop.

"Carl Conrad Coreander?"

The man giggled. "Close. I'm Mr. Brown."

Lio knew mum had a friend called Brown but never thought it was the book seller in town. His family stopped there from time to time when he was still very little and he forgot all about the old man. Now he understood why Mr. Brown's temper changed so suddenly. "So you need a book about medieval wall paintings? Ellie always liked that stuff. She used to borrow a few of them often," said Mr. Brown as he looked for the right volume.

"Is that why you didn't want to use the internet?" whispered George. Lio nodded. He meant to use the same sources as his parents to keep on their tracks.

"Did he mean Lio!rt when he called you Dragonlord?" asked George when Mr. Brown disappeared behind another bookshelf.

"Yes."

"But you're Liort!"

"Never mind." Meanwhile little puddles of water formed on the floor where they stood. Their clothes were still dripping water. "Here," said Brown when he rejoined them, "are some of the best encyclopedias I have about this topic. You can have a look at them."

"Could you tell which books mum used to borrow so often?"

Brown nodded and went back to the shelf-maze where he was out of the boys' view. George sneezed and opened one of the books. He soon found it boring and wandered around the room. This time the amount of books in Brown's hands was bigger. He put them on the table with a sigh.

Lio thanked him, dried his hands with a tissue and looked at the titles of each book. Mr. Brown sat back in his chair, taking his book, but Lio knew he was watching him. This made him nervous, but he decided to act naturally. He was surprised to find most of the books were not related at all to the painting. Most of them were fictional, including <u>The Hound of the Baskervilles</u> and <u>The Color of Magic</u>. Then there were one or two philosophy books, two encyclopedias about art and society in the Middle Ages, and then just books about different religions.

Brown noticed Lio's amazement and added, "when I suggested the Bible or the Koran to her she refused to read it." Lio browsed through one of the encyclopedias to see if he could find some useful information. A sneeze told him George was coming back his way. He didn't care about his wet clothes anymore and sat on a near chair. "By the way, what are you two doing in town?" asked Mr. Brown. "We're looking for-" "A book mum wanted. I wasn't sure which one it was, that's why I asked you for so many." said Lio before George finished the sentence. Something told him to keep the reason of their visit secret. He had no reasonable explanation for the feeling, but it was not the first time it happened to him and he had learned to obey it.

"I see. How's Ellie? And why did she send you instead of coming herself?"

Lio gasped. Mr. Brown didn't know! "She's fine," he heard himself saying with forced calmness, "but she's… busy. And we live a little far away, so it's hard to get here."

"Busy? She finally started working?"

Only now Lio remembered mum never worked. Sweat covered his forehead. He had never lied like that before. Why did he start in the first place?

"Yeah, she became a gardener," George saved him at the last moment.

Both Lio and the seller looked at him unbelievably.

"A gardener?"

"Sort of." murmured Lio who hurried to pay all his attention to the books again. Browsing in silence was embarrassing too and when George started coughing all Lio wanted to do was to jump up and tell Brown the truth. George came nearer and joined Lio. The boy chose the fiction novels.

"That's a –ehm- lot of books!" he coughed, "The Secret Garden? That's for girls. Mio, My Son, never heard of that. –ehm- The Hound of the Baskervilles, The Lord of the Rings, wow, it's heavy, The Color of Magic? This one isn't that old. Narnia, Peter Pan, The Alchemist, who would read all this?"

Suddenly a cold gust of wind sneaked inside. The door opened. Hesitated steps were heard approaching on the wooden floor. "Hello?" said a man's voice. With some difficulty Mr. Brown got to his feet and hurried to help the new customer. Only then Lio dared to take out his phone and look at the picture of the wall painting. He could find nothing similar in the encyclopedias. His spirit sank. The whole affair must have been a coincidence after all...

"Lio, I'm cold," said George.

"These books are quite easy to get anywhere," he said

more to himself. He just couldn't give up so easily. Not after this trip to town. "Why did she borrow them from this specific shop?"

"Lio, I think I have a sore throat."

"They must have something in common," *but what?* He opened a page in the phone and wrote down the names of all the books, including the date of their first publication.

"Lio…"

He sighed. They could find nothing more here. It was past lunch time. He looked around. Had there once been any windows they were now surely hidden behind book shelves and layers of dust. There was no way to know what was happening outside. He knew it was time to leave the book shop if they wanted to arrive home before dark. "Choose a book, George," he said because he already felt uncomfortable of the long visit. He picked a large one in a leather covering without a name on it. When Lio went to the entrance to pay, the glass door revealed it had stopped raining. "This month the weather's really horrible," said Mr. Brown, "last spring I painted the door green and it's already peeling."

***

Smoke stuffed the interior like a mist, hanging on the ceiling, crawling on the floor, flowing around the tables.

Loud laughter was heard from different parts of the pub, accompanied by the tinkling of glasses. Nothing was visible because of the fog. Even the faint sunbeams sneaking through the clouds outside offered a better light than the electric bulbs on the walls. A strong smell of meat and cigarettes mixed within the smoke. It was unbearable. "Ok, let's try another place," decided Lio the minute they opened the door.

They were looking for a place to eat lunch before proceeding on the way home. He turned to go, but found George stepping inside. Somewhat alarmed he forced himself to follow him and caught him by the sleeve. "I said we should try another place, George," he said and looked anxiously around. Who knows what kind of people go to such places.

"But it's cold and I'm tired." he sneezed.

"George, come outside!"

"No! I wanna stay."

With these words he went on. Lio stood at the entrance, shocked. *What got into that boy?* At last he gathered his courage and followed George to get him outside, trying to ignore the horrible smell and his urge to cough. He felt as if he was choking. Sour tears filled his eyes.

'Rest for a while, why are you beating without a break?'

He looked around. Only after some time it became clear to him, that the voice was heard only by him. It was the inner voice speaking to his heart, as it had done so many times before. "Don't bother me anymore, I have to find George."

'It is easier to think when everything is still and the mind is resting.'

"I mustn't, I have to find George and get out of here." he said almost loudly, fighting this deadly calmness. Its suggestion was tempting, very tempting that moment. How Lio wished to disappear, not to hear, not to see, not to move, not to breathe, but to escape the reality.

'Rest for a —'

"No!"

Something hitting the floor, glass breaking, a few swear words. It was George. He had dropped a roundish glass that stood on the beer-stained bar. Quick, heavy steps announced the approaching landlady. "Oh!" she said in a high voice.

"George…"

The boy fixed his gaze on his feet, "I'm sorry."

Lio turned to the lady and faced her brown eyes. "How can I repay it?"

"Oh!" she said again, "it's nothing. Sit down, we'll talk it over."

He sank into the nearest chair and she fetched another one for herself. George sat in the one at the other side of the table and tried to look sorry for breaking a cup. "What can I get you?" asked the landlady kindly.

"A cup of tea would be nice."

She disappeared from their view for a while. Then she came back with two cups of tea and a bowl of biscuits. "You need to cheer up," she explained. Lio smiled.

"Now, you can pay for three cups of tea and all is solved."

"And the biscuits…"

"Don't mind them."

He smiled again, "thank you very much."

Soon enough George forgot his little performance and devoured half the cookies. Then he noticed a small boy at another table watching him so he went to him. "They're so adorable, these children," she said, and when she noticed Lio's discomfort she added, "next year they'll forbid smoking in public places. I better rely on the law than fight with these people." He nodded.

"Won't you try to meet someone too?" asked the landlady and pointed at a couple of young women next to the window. "I guess I'll stay here."

"Are you sure you want just tea?"

"Yes."

"Well, I have to go now. Work never ends."

As Lio was left sitting alone he examined the other tables. It seemed the smoke lessened and the visitors of the pub became visible. Most of them were men, talking loudly and drinking alcohol, and there were one or two families. George gathered all the children and they sat on the floor and admired him. Lio's glance stopped at a small table in the corner. One person was sitting there, a woman. He got up slowly to see her better. She was younger than himself, about sixteen or seventeen, her slim figure wrapped in a winter coat. Her thick brown hair cascaded down her shoulders. There was nothing special about her, but for some reason Lio felt she didn't belong there. As if she was taken from another world and seated here by accident.

His heart started beating quicker than ever. It was her.

He realized he was moving towards her table. Step after step he came nearer. He tried to stop, to persuade himself she was only a vision, but his heart ignored reason. His feet brought him to the chair facing her. Slowly he sat down and then she looked at him. "Hello, Liort," she said in her quiet voice. She said the same words once before. This time Lio wouldn't let her go. His hand reached her before he could stop to think. He grasped her arm. "Don't go."

A slight smile slowly appeared on her lips. "I won't."

They didn't move for a long time. Then Lio left her hand, a little worried of what would come next. She stayed in her seat, showing no sign of leaving. Another long period of silence passed. All this time his eyes were fixed upon her, as if he could hope to hold her by his gaze. He winced when she held out her hand. He heard a tinkling sound as she passed a few coins to his hand. "Pay for the tea and buy some food to take with you. We should have been on our way by now."

Lio was completely stunned but obeyed. George joined him at the bar and was glad to see that Lio did buy some food. However, when he saw the girl at the table that his brother was going towards, he stopped about two meters from her, holding Lio's hand tightly. "Hi," he said at last.

"Hi, George," she answered. Neither of the boys moved, nor knew what to do. It was probably the first time Lio felt they shared the same feeling, and it wasn't a good one. She understood no action was going to be taken on their part, so she walked towards the door herself. Still holding George's hand, Lio followed her, taking the book and the food. She led them to the train station, and bought three tickets in the direction of their village.

No one sat in the coupe except for them. When the train started moving Lio took out his wallet in an attempt to give the girl back the money, but she shook her head.

"Who are you?" he asked in a low voice.

"You don't know." This startled him a little. It wasn't a question, it was an announcement. He didn't answer.

"But I know who you are," she said. The chugging of the train was the only noise disturbing the silence for a few minutes. Then she broke the silence again. "I know why you came to town. I know what you're looking for."

"You know too much," whispered George, "or you pretend to know too much."

Her soft laughter chimed through the air. "I know it may look weird."

"Well I know that you forgot to tell us who you are," cried George. Lio didn't stop him. He was glad he wasn't the one who had to start the argument.

"I'll tell you. But not yet."

George wouldn't give up so quickly. He asked all the questions that came into his mind including how she liked the town and how was the weather yesterday, but she remained silent. Lio didn't speak either. At last George saw he could do nothing about it and none of them said a word for the rest of the ride.

***

Heavy rain awaited them at their arrival. Gravel on the path to the village was carried downhill by streams of water, jumping, rolling, and running. It looked as if the path gravel was transformed by some magic into small creatures that chatted and laughed and splashed water in all direction around their tiny feet along their long race. Sometimes the little stones would run in pairs, talking all the way, then jumping over a tiny puddle that separated them, finding new companions, forgetting that the one they had lost was someone else. It would go on and on until the sky cleared and the clouds would be blown away and the sun would come out to dry the little stones, but the little creatures were disturbed after all by the steps of six feet hitting the ground.

The gravel stones looked up to see the far away faces of the intruders. They saw it was a boy, a young man, and a girl, each knowing nothing about the creatures below. Then the gravel stones shrugged their tiny shoulders, renewed the lively conversation and ran alongside with the three travelers returning home.

Lio was glad to breathe clean air again. He was always more confident when there were less people nearby. He took great care not to lose sight of the girl. He started to believe that she had something to do with the mystery of his parents. Maybe that was why she knew so much. Water started to fill the plastic bag in his hand. They finished all the food from the pub, but the book from Mr. Brown's bookshop was inside. Lio tried to pour the water out and closed it better in order to protect the old volume which was in bad condition anyway. George walked behind them. That was a bit odd, for it was usually Lio who walked behind. About half the way the girl stopped and opened her handbag.

"Oh dear," she said, "I knew I had an umbrella." They

indeed found the journey easier under the safe shelter of the umbrella. They arrived at the circle of houses and turned to the direction of their house. The young woman knew the way perfectly as if she had followed this path more often than Lio himself. The house appeared in front of them when she suddenly caught Lio's arm and dragged him to the wall of the nearest building.

He wanted to protest and ask what had happened, but she signed to him to be quiet. George ran to them. They leaned on the wall, she was looking at the house from behind the building. It was obvious they were hiding. But why? "They're here," she whispered.

"Who?" George said, fisting his hands, "what are you talking about?"

Again she raised her finger to her lips and pointed at the house. At first Lio couldn't understand what made her act the way she did. He watched the house for a moment, trying to find a reasonable explanation. Nothing. At last he gave up and turned back to the house when something caught his attention. It was the air, the wind. He noticed it was glittering. When he forced his eyes to focus on it, he saw that the breeze became visible. Slowly blue and green colors in the sky became apparent. The colors moved and mixed without a break, dancing with the rain in the silence. Their hue was so faint he wouldn't have seen it had she not warned him.

"What is it?" he whispered.

"What?" said George, trying to escape the girl's hold to step back on the path and have a better look. "There's nothing!"

"Don't you see the colors?" Lio uttered.

"What colors?" George gave up on whispering. He was getting angry.

"They were quicker than I thought," she whispered, "we can't go there. Not yet."

"But who?" asked Lio.

"They don't have a name, we call them spirits."

"How didn't I notice it before?"

"Because they weren't here before."

George folded his arms, "you're not funny. My throat is sore. Let's go home."

"George, look closely," said Lio, "it's blue, and green!"

"It's more likely your nose is blue and green than the house!"

Lio looked at the colors, then at her, then at George. He shivered. George really saw nothing of all this. *What was that supposed to mean? Why couldn't they go home? How come he could see it if George couldn't? How was she related to all this?*

"Do you have another place to stay?" She turned to Lio. He didn't answer for a while. "Actually, yes."

Running up the hill to the white house was never easy because of the soft ground, but running up the hill in the rain with a head full of questions was even more difficult. The three of them arrived panting and wet. Lio knocked on the door. Miss Rose opened. Her wrinkled face revealed her amazement. "George?" she whispered. But her eyes were fixed on the girl. "Nice to see you again, Jane," she said.

***

"Be careful, it's hot." They were sitting in Miss Rose's living room, close to the radiator and drinking tea. Their wet clothes were hanging in the bathroom to dry, meanwhile Miss Rose brought them old ones that she kept in the attic. The atmosphere wasn't exactly positive.

Everything was silent except for an occasional sneeze from George. "You look sick," said Miss Rose at last, "come, we'll make your bed." He nodded and ran to the upper floor where his bedroom used to be. The old woman followed him.

"So," said Lio when he and the girl were left alone for a while, "your name is… George?" She nodded. Her eyes were fixed on him which made him uncomfortable. "Was it…" his voice cracked in the middle of the sentence. He tried again. "Was it you who wrote letters to my parents?"

Another nod.

"But… how? It was before I was even born."

"Right," she smiled.

"You seem younger than me!"

She leaned back in her armchair. "Don't judge people by their appearance."

He wanted to ask more, but Miss Rose came back. The girl used the opportunity and got up. "Thank you, Jane, I think I'll also go to bed now. It's been a long day."

"Won't you have dinner first?"

"No, thanks. I'm not hungry." With these words she left.

Lio followed her with his eyes until she disappeared behind the door. This was the person who wrote secret messages to his parents. It was so impossible to understand. It must have been a mistake. He jumped up to follow her, but then fell on the chair again. What if it was true after all? He had so many questions that he didn't know what he would ask her exactly. And the name… George…

Miss Rose noticed his mixed feelings. She put her creased hand on his shoulder. "Who is she?" he whispered.

"I don't really know," her voice taking on the sweet tone it always had when she tried to calm Lio down, "but she is a powerful person."

"You know her." Miss Rose sighed, "Sometimes she appears at some place or another. When George comes it's either a good or a bad sign. Anyway, she always comes to help."

She was quiet for a while. "She helped your father too," she said at last. Lio bit his lips. He was trembling. *How could be that called help?* With shivering fingers he took the last letter from his mother's box and handed it to the old lady. "What is it?"

"Skip two words."

When she read the message she gasped and fell on the nearest chair. He smiled bitterly. "Oh, Liort! I didn't know…" He found it impossible to speak. He felt he was about to cry. But he wouldn't. Not now. He got up and went upstairs too, leaving Miss Rose alone.

The door of his brother's room was open. George was already sleeping, hugging the pillow instead of lying on it. Lio closed the door carefully. Then he went to his room and sat on the bed. It's been a long time since he was in that room. At least two years. He never knew how much he missed it. Through the open window he could see the darkness hanging over the land outside like a curtain, marked by thousands of shining diamonds. They danced from one corner of the sky to the other, winking occasionally at someone down there. He hoped it was him. His troubles were big enough to shine like a little gem to the stars to attract their favor. That's what he thought stars do, mirror the tiny diamonds on the ground. To donate hope. They winked again, or at least he imagined they did.

Lio had hope, he really did. Hopefully, the girl could tell him everything. Miss Rose said she was there to help. The question was what kind of help she could give. He shivered. How would it be? To get to know what and why happened, after all those years? The memory of the colored wind surrounding his house arose in his mind. Perhaps his task wasn't only to find out the truth about his parents. Perhaps something awaited him. What? Why?

It was so simple. The answer awaited him next door, but he just couldn't do it. He feared it too much. The feelings he had felt as a boy in the very same room entered him. The disappointment, the sadness, the hopelessness. He was troubled back then, troubled and worried. These feelings grew every year, taking control over him. He knew he suffered. Lio discovered with horror that although there was nothing he would wish more, he didn't dare to try the cure.

"Not yet," he said, "not yet." He laid down, slowed his breath and thought about other things. Despite trying his eyes wouldn't close. They would wander across the room to the opposite wall. The wall which she was behind. He shook his head and reached for the first book he saw. It was the one from Brown's shop. He opened it, taking care not to tear out the old pages. It took him a while to take a look at the first page, for he still found it impossible to concentrate. Large, adorned letters gazed out onto the reader from the yellow page. Lio was surprised to see the words were in Latin.

<u>Malleus Maleficarum</u>.

A book in Latin? What could mum do with something like that? Curiosity afforded him courage. He got up, still a little hesitating, and left his room. He stopped in front of her door. Fear crawled through him. What if she wasn't there at all? When he opened George's room carefully a short glance showed him that the boy was still sleeping. Lio decided that was his chance. He didn't knock. He entered.

The window here was open as well, revealing burning squares of light that said, 'we are the village, don't forget us,' before turning off the lights to sleep. On the left side of the window stood a wardrobe with the doors proudly open. Only then Lio turned his eyes to the right side of the room, the one where the bed stood. He was so tense that had to bite his tongue when he saw her. She was sitting on the bed, still wearing the jeans and sweater Miss Rose had lent her. She smiled at him.

"I expected you to come."

He didn't know what to say. All the questions he wanted to ask escaped his memory and he stood helplessly where he was. "Sit down," she said, tapping on the bed. He obeyed automatically. There was something in her voice, in the manner of her speech that made him listen.

"Ask, I'll answer anything."

His mouth opened and closed a few times without making any sound. He bit his lips.

"You may call me Georgiana if it makes it easier for you."

At last the words came out, "Is this your full name?"

"No, I'm George."

"Oh…"

She said nothing more, giving him time to organize his thoughts.

"What…" he started once again, "what's all this about?"

"What do you mean?"

"Well," Lio found it hard to continue. He waited for a while, "they're gone and… we were alone all this time, but now…" he fixed his eyes on his feet, "they wanted us to find those letters. To look for an explanation."

Georgiana's gaze was lying on him like a heavy burden. "And those books, and you, they knew it would happen."

"There's no need to ask about what you already know."

"But why did they leave? Where are they? And why did they have to come back into our lives in such a way? Why should we know at all? Is there something George and I have to do about that?" She leaned so close to him he could feel her perfume. "It's not only about your parents, Liort. You almost found out part of the answer without me."

He became more confused than ever. What had he found out? Was it the painting? The letters? There was no answer in these things. Then there was Mr. Brown's bookshop. Was the answer hidden in the books after all? He took out his phone and opened the list he made in town.

There seemed to be no connection between the publication dates. Every book was by a different author. It was known that the author of <u>The Lord of the Rings</u> and the author of <u>Narnia</u> knew each other, but what about the others?

Lio tried to summarize the plots of the stories, to see if they had something in common after all.

He had never read <u>The Secret Garden,</u> but he had heard it was about a girl coming to England after her parents died and finding a secret garden. She takes care of it with two friends. One of them who had been ill all his life magically heals thanks to their secret.

He shook his head. This story wasn't related to his parents' life. He looked at the other titles. Mio, my Son was about a boy freeing an enchanted country by the famous author Astrid Lindgren.

The Hound of the Baskervilles, The Lord of the Rings, Narnia, and Peter Pan were all well known to him, as well as The Color of…

Suddenly he realized those books did have something in common. But this…? He skipped to Google, looking for a summary of each one. The Secret Garden, Mio, my son, The Hound of the Baskervilles, The Alchemist, The Lord of the Rings, The Chronicles of Narnia, Peter Pan, The Color of…

The name of the last book appeared in his mind: Malleus Maleficarum. Hammer of witches. This was the first proof. The second one was The Color of…

"Magic?" he whispered.

"You may call it that, yes." The window, the wardrobe and the ceiling all spun around him like a huge carousel. "Why am I supposed to believe such a thing?"

"Because it's true."

The last lights outside turned off. His strength was leaving him. It can't be, he said to himself. It's ridiculous. A few stars floated through the window to the room, dancing in front of him. He stuck to the only bit of reason he could think of. George. He wouldn't believe her so easily. *What would George say?* "This is a joke, right?" he murmured.

Her soft laughter mixed with his visions, "it's not a joke, Liort. I'll get you something to eat, you look pale."

He heard her leaving the room. Then he blinked, changing from the real blackness to the one within himself, but soon changed his mind and turned the lamp on. Light showed things the way they really were. Although the light did not make their conversation disappear.

Why am I supposed to believe such a thing?

Because it's true.

Georgiana returned with a bar of chocolate. He immediately felt better. Chocolate always made him feel better. "What do you mean, magic?" he asked after eating about a third of the bar.

"You'll understand when you'll get used to the idea."

"What does this have to do with mum and dad?"

"Most people don't know about the magic. Your parents do."

"So?" Lio noticed he was shouting, "what does it have to do with them?"

"Magic is everywhere, Liort, but most people can't see it. That's why it's dangerous for those who do."

He jumped up, "can't you just tell me instead of those riddles? I'm sick of it!"

Georgiana remained perfectly calm. She handed him the <u>Malleus Maleficarum</u>. "That's the danger. People, not magic itself. They've always been the danger and the Middle Ages are a good example of that." Lio took a deep breath. She was mad, there was no other explanation. "These women weren't real witches. They were chased only because the church had nothing better to do."

"What do you think was the reason for this chase? Magic. They could see it, they understood the world better than the others."

"There aren't witches!"

"I never called them witches."

He didn't answer.

"Think of the spirits we saw at your house. Did George see them?"

This struck him. She was right. He sat down slowly, feeling like a scolded child. She got up and, not minding Lio, took off her clothes and changed into a pajamas she found in the wardrobe. "Besides, George always overlooked things you could see."

"You want to say I'm some kind of a wizard?"

"Don't be silly. There's no such thing." She broke off a piece of chocolate and started licking it noisily.

"I don't understand."

"Why not? Chiming leaves, mirror stars, running gravel, that's all magic."

He could feel his heartbeat in his throat. How did she know what he was thinking about?

"It's only a personification. My stupid ideas. I only make up poems."

She smiled, still licking the sweet chocolate that was as brown as her large eyes. "It's not stupid. Do you believe in what you write?"

"Well, of course I do. Otherwise I wouldn't be able to write it down,"

"See? I've told you before you believe in things because they're true."

He saw no sense in her words. Disappointment mixed with his anger and fear. Georgiana watched him for a while. At last she took the rest of the chocolate and explained with a full mouth, "your dad is one of those who know about magic. I contacted him when he was about thirty. Everything went on quite well until his wife found out he was one of them. He told her his secret and soon she learned to notice the magic surrounding her too. They both did a great job keeping magic secret and hiding some of the biggest evidence. But then the spirits discovered them and the only way I could help them was to suggest to move away, somewhere where they won't be found."

"Why did they have to conceal magic?" Lio whispered.

"Mostly because of other people. When they learn the truth they become aggressive. And because of the spirits."

"Spirits?" he gasped. The colored wind floating around his house arose in his memory.

"The original guardians of magic, of laws of nature. They are against anyone knowing the secret, and try to get rid of the magicians."

Lio started shivering violently. He couldn't be a magician. His parents couldn't be magicians either. All his life he was told that magic was something impossible, unnatural, not a law of nature. Did the spirits want to kill him also? How was Georgiana connected to this absurd theory? And what about George? And above all: was this a good reason for his parents to leave their children forever?

"Go to bed," he heard her quiet voice, as if from a huge distance, "it's late." He heard the bedsheets rustle as he got up and walked towards the door. He didn't say anything. He exited. He was half asleep by the time he reached his room. The clean smell of roses awaited him in his old bed, it relaxed his eyes and repelled the thoughts of the confused events. His mind cleared except for the words that circled around his conscience again and again as a reminder of the connection between his past and present.

'The supply of game for London is going steadily up. Head keeper Hudson, we believe, has been now told to receive all orders for fly-paper and for preservation of your hen-pheasant's life.'

***

The darkness makes me feel

Alone, so lone and frail.

While they're outside forgetting

The sadness rain is tatting.

And immense avalanches,

Tumultuously falling down.

While they are climbing tree branches

To get closer to the sun...

"Breakfast's ready." To Lio's surprise it wasn't Miss Rose calling him, but Georgiana. She was standing at the top of the stairs with bare feet, waiting for him to join her. He hurried to do so. He had been wondering about their conversation since he woke up. Lio came to the conclusion it must have been nothing more than a dream. It wasn't the first time a nonsensical idea with no sense had become highly important in one from his dreams. Somewhat satisfied he started writing a new poem. He had enough books for the last few days.

"And by the way," added Georgiana as they went down the stairs, "I wouldn't write poems now, it could draw the spirits' attention and we don't want that." He froze in his place, and just watched her in disbelief as she went to the dining room. "You coming?" He heard her voice after a short while.

Miss Rose and little George were already seated at the table, with four bowls of hot porridge in front of them. This, and his red nose, was a clear sign that George wasn't feeling well. It was Miss Rose's habit, whenever anyone got ill to cook his favorite food. Lio thought it was nice and caring, although he disliked that mush that gazed at him like an old enemy from the bowl. He sighed.

"You really shouldn't have gone outside yesterday, Liort," Miss Rose started her lecture, "now poor George is all feverish." She continued judging Lio's actions while George, who wasn't the poor boy she said he was at all that moment as he produced innocent smiles behind her back.

"I'm sorry," Lio interrupted her, "I didn't expect this to happen. After all, I'm not his dad to watch every step of his."

"No, but you're responsible for him. Unless you leave him to my care." The conversation stopped thanks to Georgiana, who had changed the topic.

After breakfast the old lady insisted upon washing the dishes alone. She seated the three of them in the living room.

"You don't like porridge," observed Georgiana.

Lio shook his head. "But at least I don't have to cook."

"Don't you like cooking?"

"I'm not good at that and I avoid it as much as I can."

"That's not true," said George lifting up his large green eyes, "I like Lio's pancakes."

Georgiana laughed and Lio allowed himself to smile. "Thanks."

Slowly the faded silhouette of the sun behind the clouds rose, climbing up to the center of the sky. There it paused, shimmering like a reflection in a deep lake, resting before its journey continued. Lio ran to his room to get the pencil and notebook and put on his coat. Georgiana joined him at the entrance.

"Where are you going?" cried Miss Rose from the other room.

"To the publishing house."

"Don't forget the umbrella, I don't want you to be sick too." He reached for it, but the girl stopped him, taking out her own umbrella. "I'm coming with you."

Lio couldn't force himself to argue anymore and they left the house. He tried to ignore Georgiana. Her presence was still somewhat unnerving and unwelcome. Lio looked the other way, at the houses, at the street lights, and the short garden walls. He observed the trees, the distant hills, and the people passing by. This was his inspiration. Such a small place full of so many things, revealed as well as hidden everywhere. This was what he knew, the source of all his thoughts, the reason of his being. Even on a cloudy day, life in the village would go on, it would fight to live its own way and no other, and Lio felt he had every reason to be proud of belonging there.

He was interrupted by a slight push. Georgiana took the

notebook from his hands. She listed and read a few poems. A smile appeared on her thin lips in what seemed to be appreciation. She didn't say anything for quite a long time, letting the words subside in her mind. "They're good," she said at last, "this one is very effective," she pointed at *'Goes My Song.'* A deep feeling of satisfaction warmed him within. These were the exact words he had longed to hear for such a long time.

"Your words are very complicated," she added, "don't you want to write easier poems?" The lovely feeling left him immediately and he became offended instead. Lio grabbed his notebook, just about to continue walking, when he saw how sincere her face was. She didn't mean to insult him. He decided to continue their conversation. He opened the notebook and scribbled four lines:

Roses are red,

Violets are blue,

This is the thing

I will never do.

"Why not?" she asked after finishing reading.

Roses can tear,

Violets always rot,

These poems sound stupid,

Especially when they're short.

"Oh, I see," she laughed. Lio closed the notebook and went on. Gravel and sand cracked beneath their feet as they walked along the road. Lio gazed at the horizon, trying desperately to get ideas.

Think of… rain, he told himself, *rain, rainy, raindrop, rainbow…*

"Listen," cried Georgiana at last and ran to catch him, "I wouldn't publish those poems now,"

He bit his lip, but didn't stop. She caught him by the arm. "You shouldn't do that, Liort!"

"Why not?" he cried, "why? You drove my family out of my life, then suddenly you decided it was a good idea to appear, yesterday you scared me with some nonsense about witchcraft, and now you tell me how to earn my money? Isn't it enough?"

She wanted to respond, but Lio wouldn't let her, "these

poems are the only thing I can do. They exist because of me, I exist because of them. You cannot and will not take them away too."

"You're right," she whispered, still holding his hand, "Liort, you are a magician, you know you are, and your words are your power. There's nothing I respect more than that. But the spirits can feel it too, so it's too risky to exhibit them like that. They're on our track so we need to be careful." Suddenly he forgot his anger, and turned to lightheartedness. He smiled, giggled, and laughed. Soon he laughed so hard that he fell on the road, holding his stomach. "What," he gasped, "what on Earth are you talking about?"

It was evident she was hardly controlling herself. She took a deep breath, "It's not that I decided to come to you all of a sudden and claim you're a magician just like that, because I wanted to, Liort. I knew about you all this time, since you were less than three years old, exactly as I know about all the others. I contact all the magicians when they're ready and that's when they're about thirty or more,"

"I'm twenty one," Lio cut her off.

"I know. I'm not here only because of you, as are the spirits."

"Why then?" she lowered her tone, "as a magician you

should know that, use your words to think." Lio looked into her chocolate eyes. He understood. This was the test, this was his way of proving her wrong. All right. He glanced at the raindrops, at the landscape. Then he started making up a poem. A poem with his words.

Lio looked at the heavy rain drops hitting the ground. *Heavy rain is falling,* Then his eyes focused on the landscape. *Far away, in that land with no end.* He saw Miss Rose's house, the fact that she had known Georgiana all these years still shocked him. *Secret names calling,* automatically, he suppressed these thoughts. He looked at the garden. George was sitting outside. *As no one witnesses, but green-*

Suddenly Lio stopped. The view of this empty place with only is brother outside made him uncomfortable. He tried to continue his poem but couldn't. Every time he ended up thinking about little George alone in the rain. It probably meant something. *Could it be…? No.* In spite of his tries he asked, "George?" For some reason Lio knew it was the right answer. "What has George done?"

"Nothing," she seemed relieved, her body became less tensed, "he's growing up."

"So?" Lio recalled her words from the day before, "you

said he wasn't a magician, that he couldn't see things I saw,"

"No, he's not a magician, he's like me."

"What?" The more she told him about the topic the more confused he was. His reasoning told him that she must have been crazy, but still something in his heart made him believe her. Doubt entered him. Should he tell Miss Rose? Should he not take her seriously but rather listen just to calm Georgiana down? No, he knew he would memorize every word.

Suddenly she pulled him off the road, holding him by the sleeve just before a jeep's wheels ran over the place where they had been sitting. "Careful." They continued walking. Lio let her lead, he didn't know where they were going. He found himself following her to the old mill. His surprise didn't last long, as he assumed that Georgiana already knew about the drawing he had found; and indeed she walked straight to it.

"Look. Do you know what this is?" she said after a long while. With some difficulty Lio overcame his anger and answered. "A medieval painting."

"It's only styled like one. The paint wouldn't have lasted so long in such a good condition. Still, it's quite old." Her thin finger ran down the rough bricks, "the mill was built around this wall about eighty years ago. When the painting was drawn it still belonged to a tiny chapel, ruined a long time ago." She paused for a second. Then she quickly glanced at Lio. "Do you know what they mean?"

"What?"

"The scenes in the painting. Do you know what they mean?"

He shook his head reluctantly.

"These people are gods and heroes of many cultures," she pointed at various figures as if to clarify, "Christian, Muslim, Buddhist, Hindu, Jewish, and more."

"This is impossible, Europeans didn't know about other cultures back then," protested Lio.

"They did. There's no doubt about that. This painting is special because they don't fight." It was true. Figures dressed in different styles and colors were sitting together in perfect peace, holding hands, or even hugging. The only paintings involving more than one culture, Lio remembered, were scenes from famous battles. The next thing he noticed, which he had previously overlooked was a tiny circle above each scene, hanging in the air like a lamp illuminating the motionless figures. Georgiana's finger rested on one of the circles.

"This represents the reason of their peace, the sign of magic. Of perfect balance, including everything and everyone without considering culture, religion, or money. This is the only thing that is the same for everyone. The fact that autumn follows summer, that rain fills rivers, that rivers always reach the sea, that the sea is deeper than human understanding, mightier than our power. The fact that there is always something natural, bigger than ourselves, holds us together. You don't need to belong to a certain culture to know these things. This is what makes people understand we're all basically the same."

Lio's voice cracked as he spoke, "then why do magicians keep all this secret?"

 "Because people want to be different, to be unique, to lie about other cultures to gain power. Peace doesn't make such power, such money as war does. If one person started talking about magic too much the blind crowd would attack him, and stomp on him until his words fade and his thoughts fade with them; and yet, we mustn't let the magic be forgotten. If we did, we'd ruin the balance, and the spirits would freely bend magic as they please and we'd forget how things should really be."

"I don't think that could ever happen."

Her gaze fixed on him, breaking his confidence into

pieces. "It is happening already. Why do you think it's not snowing this winter? Why do you think we don't stop this global warming? We're starting to forget how good winters used to be, those good, snowy winters. You magicians have to hide the magic, but still reveal it to others little by little to keep the world the way it is supposed to be."

Georgiana continued, "just to make it clear, a magician isn't that sort of thing like in movies and fantasy books and I don't know what else. Nothing abnormal. You're spread all over the world, but there's less of you each year. Then there are the spirits," she lowered her voice, "and then there's me. I keep an eye on the magicians and help them when there's trouble. Most often when the spirits come. And it's my job to tell them about their abilities."

"And George? What does he have to do with all this?" asked Lio.

She leaned to him, breaking the invisible barrier between him and the rest of the world. He started feeling terribly uncomfortable. "He will succeed me."

Lio shivered. No matter how odd her words seemed to him he believed her, because it was true. He turned around and continued walking, back to Miss Rose's house. Georgiana stayed behind, calling his name, but he didn't care.

***

Lio spent the whole morning before lunch helping Miss Rose in her garden. Luckily there was no sign of rain, but the storm from the day before had broken off many branches that were now lying on the ground, blocking the walkway to the entrance. The weather was so cold that he soon couldn't feel his fingers. When they finished and Miss Rose went back inside to make lunch he just continued walking around the house with nothing to do.

At last George called him for lunch in a hoarse voice, of course not without laughing about Lio's ridiculous behavior. He didn't touch his food. Georgiana didn't mention their talk, but hurried to disappear to her room as soon as she could to leave the others alone. Lio wondered about how well she understood him, unlike most people.

"You have to eat at least something, Liort," said Miss Rose from the kitchen as she washed her plate. "I'm not hungry," he murmured.

"I know why Lio's behaving so strangely," said George with a mischievous smile, "he's in love with George!"

"No I'm not," cried Lio. He knew he was angrier than he was supposed to be and only supported George, but he couldn't conceal his feelings now. "I don't believe anyone could fall in love with someone like her."

"Come on, admit it," the boy laughed, "she's pretty and she has a beautiful name."

"That's enough, George," said Miss Rose, "if Liort's not hungry he can eat later."

Lio thanked her and hurried to leave the room before George could say anything else. He went to Georgiana's room. He knew she expected him. She was sitting on her bed, reading a book. She didn't put it down when Lio entered. He had as much time as he needed. "You said George will succeed you," he uttered at last.

"Yes."

"Succeed what?"

She raised her eyes, looking deep into his. "Representing the magicians' side."

"The good side?"

"I never said spirits were bad." He sat down, not next to her, but on the floor, leaning his back on the wall.

"What are spirits?"

"Something similar to what the books and movies call magic," suddenly she looked sad, "they can do… unbelievable things."

"But are they alive at all?" asked Lio.

"That's exactly the difference between us. We come and go. But they- they stay. These are the same spirits as millions of years ago. But then there's a tricky part: a magician can turn into a spirit if he chooses to." Lio felt he was loosing the sense of the whole conversation again. "I don't understand."

"When a magician chooses to use magic he becomes a spirit. That is why there are two sides. Both protect magic, but only one is against using it."

"You mean to say there's war between them."

"No, only a never ending argument leading to a bloodshed."

He bit his lips, "what if I don't want to be part of it?"

"You don't have to," Georgiana smiled, "you can always choose."

This calmed him down a little. He knew Georgiana

wouldn't make up anything regarding this matter. There were no lies between them. "And you?"

"I was more limited." she answered and got up, playing with her hair, "I was about ten years old when I could've accepted to take my role or continue living as before. I didn't really know what I was doing," she smiled, "but I don't regret it."

"You started traveling around the world, looking for magicians all alone with no place to stay when you were ten years old?" His tone was more sarcastic than serious.

"Of course not. I started when I was seventeen. And I wasn't alone, I was with George."

"With…" Lio shook his head. "Oh I see, the one before you was called George too."

She nodded. "But there are thousands of Georges all over the world!"

"And only one of them is the right one."

"Do you really think such a disorganized boy as my George could live with no one to help him and with no home? To make decisions that could effect many lives? And to do it with awareness and responsibility?" he cried.

"I can teach him how." The silence that followed was so

thick that it was possible to feel it in the space between them. Georgiana was the one who broke it. "You know you're not the one who has to take care of him. You could have left it to Jane. Now you can leave it to me."

A strange smile spread across his face. He remembered all the recent events since he had deciphered those letters, and then the moment his parents left, and then he thought how his entire life that had been a lie. Then there was George: a naive, bright dot of light in the dark. The burning torch inspiring him to go on, the reason Lio didn't give up in the very beginning of his journey.

"You're almost grown up, Liort," recalled the voice within him of his father's words, *"you're ready to take care of George."* "I will never give up on him."

"Well," said Georgiana on her way to leave the room, "then I'm lucky it's not up to you."

***

He spent the rest of the day near his house, sitting on the wet grass and watching the spirits floating with the wind in unusual calmness. Their beauty was enchanting, they kept moving and changing in an exotic way, and yet, something about them was hurting his eyes. He could feel it wasn't only a spectacle, but that they were alive. Lio felt something towards them, deep inside where his logical thinking had lost all power over him, but he couldn't call it sympathy. At last darkness covered the village and his coat couldn't protect him from the cold. He got up to leave. Only then he realized his legs hurt from sitting so long. Lio started jumping up and down to get warmer and tucked his hands in his pockets. There was a folded piece of paper. It took him a while to see that these were the deciphered messages. He was just about to fold it again but changed his mind and looked at the last one.

'Leave at once. miss rose will take care of the boys. meet as usual.

George.'

Lio still couldn't believe that all this was happening only because of the spirits. There was something dangerous about them, but there must have been another, more reasonable explanation. A good parent would never abandon his children just to save his own life.

Lio thought of all the things Georgiana had told him. Slowly she revealed a world that was so different from all he had ever known.

Spirits and magicians were trapped in a never ending argument. The spirits tried to get rid of the magicians.

The magicians couldn't get rid of the spirits, but they had something the other side didn't have: Georgiana. A representative thanks to whom it all worked. It was hard for Lio to persuade himself that all of this was indeed true. He decided to act as if it was, for now. He knew his parents left because the spirits had found them. But if Lio was in the spirits' place he wouldn't chase magicians. He would chase Georgiana. If Georgiana disappeared before finding someone to succeed her all the magicians' side would collapse.

Lio threw another look towards the house, but it was already hidden by the night. He arrived to the road and walked by its side, not forgetting to beware of cars. However, he continued with his theories, Georgiana was now here claiming that George, his brother, would assume her role. She also said Lio and his father were magicians. Was it only a terrible coincidence? Did dad know?

Lio suddenly stopped. Of course dad knew about him and George! A good parent would never abandon his children just to save his own life, he would take them with him. That is the reason mum and dad had left, leaving him and George behind! So that the spirits would pursue them instead of George!

Dark clouds gathered above him, dropping ribbons of light and pearls of liquid glass while making the horrifying noises of a storm. Lio looked up, crying and smiling at the same time. He was… he was relieved. The heavy burden that hung over him all those years disappeared, the chain vanished. At last he knew the answer to the question he had asked over and over again. And Lio believed this answer with all his heart, because it was true. "My ears are void," he shouted to the clouds and to the rain and to the noise, "but I am glad, it was my choice."

***

"I've had the strangest dream," said George. Lio opened his eyes. This time his brother didn't wake him, he had just come back inside from the storm. His hair was wet and his clothes were dirty with mud but he lay on the bed anyway. Suddenly the tiny room seemed to him much bigger, more… airy. "I've had a dream," repeated the boy.

"Of course you had." said Lio calmly. He expected George would come.

"I've dreamed you went outside. And then you stood in the rain in that darkness and laughed." he continued. "That did happen George."

"And then you suddenly found a way leading somewhere."

Lio sat up. He examined his brother, sitting on the floor in his pajamas and reddish nose. Now he knew he should take George more seriously. "What did I find, George? Where did the way lead?" "I don't know, you found it." He watched him with his big green eyes until Lio made a place for him on the bed. Then they sat side by side, piercing the opposite wall with their gaze. Lio breathed loudly, soaking in bigger amounts of air than ever before. He felt as though he could just get up and start floating in the air, ignoring gravity. He felt free; free and self-confident. The feeling was almost new to him. Lio reached for a piece of paper and a pen.

Soon enough George became clearly tired of watching him writing and started to wander around the room. After he explored all he could he simply opened the door and left. Lio was surprised to hear George's quick, heavy steps were going in the opposite direction from his own room. After a while it occurred to him that George was heading to Georgiana's room. Whether it was only because of his sleepiness or on purpose was hard to tell.

He guessed they would talk, she and his brother, and she would tell him everything. He knew George would take it very easily and follow her blindly as if it was a game. His feeling of freedom abandoned him for a second and an urge to stop George made him burst into the corridor. He was just in time to see George's leg disappear behind the door. Lio realized how nauseous he was feeling and so he let George go. After all, he didn't want to be the one to tell him, so he hobbled back to his room.

Without even noticing, words and memories appeared in his mind. Good, snowy winters: *wild*, a quiet Christmas by the fireplace: *hope*, the present he got on his fourteenth birthday, a crystal snow ball: *ice*, inside the ball were tiny mountains that stood proudly in the miniature storm: *hills*, the vast fields near their house: *land*, and then the memory of all the times he was truly happy.

The pictures in his memory disappeared when he opened his eyes. On the paper he held in front of him lay the words:

My voice goes on, my hope will rise

In the wild land of hills and ice.

Lio had absolutely no idea what it meant. "George!" The cry came from the other room. Lio ran to the corridor with the paper in his hand to find Georgiana running to him and his brother following her. It was George who called her. Lio hesitated and stopped where he was. She looked worried. It must have been a bad sign. "You found it," she said. He gave her an obtuse look. He noted that she was actually much shorter than she seemed before, her head only reached his shoulder.

Georgiana checked that the windows were closed and then said in a low voice, "I told George everything. You were writing something, weren't you?" He nodded. "You understood why they left." It was clear what she meant. He nodded again. Meanwhile George rubbed his eyes and continued wandering around. "You just discovered where they are." "No, I…" his eyes wandered to the paper in his hand.

My voice goes on, my hope will rise

In the wild land of hills and ice.

"A wild land… with hills and ice…" he murmured. George suddenly entered Georgiana's rooms and exited again. He was biting his nails, throwing worried glances towards the windows.

"My hope will rise… hills and ice…" The boy started jumping up and down, then sat down, then got up again, then did it all over. "Land, ice…" He felt George grabbing his hand. "Someone's following us."

"Iceland." He didn't need Georgiana to prove him right. Their parents were in Iceland. Suddenly he became nauseous again and he vomited before he could stop himself. He barely heard George jumping back and calling his name. Their parents were in Iceland.

The next moment Miss Rose was there, talking to him and caressing his hair, but he couldn't understand a word. He realized he was on the floor. Georgiana was sitting next to him, George was out of sight again. Their parents were in Iceland. This was the only thing he could think about.

George ran back into the corridor. "Someone's following us!" he cried. Lio sat up. "The spirits," he said. He began to understand what was happening. "Yes," Georgiana's tone was very nervous too. "We have to go."

"What are you talking about, dears?" cried Miss Rose. Lio smiled at her. It wasn't one of those smiles to satisfy her, he smiled because he was happy; nervous, nauseous, but happy. "We're going to see mum and dad." Miss Rose was too stunned to say anything.

"I'll get a taxi, you pack what you need, quickly." uttered Georgiana as she hurried downstairs. She stepped in the vomit on the floor, but she ignored it. Lio hurried to his room. He grabbed his poems, blank papers, a pencil, and the phone. There was nothing else he needed. He looked at the stars outside and took a deep breath, a truly deep one.

"Are you OK, Lio?" It was George. He was standing in the door with a bundle of toys in his hands.

Lio laughed, "I'm better than ever."

"Aren't you mad at mum and dad?"

"I am."

"Then why are you laughing?"

"Because I missed them too."

George hesitated, then he put his toys on the floor. "I know you do." Lio waited for him to continue. "Did George tell you? I'm an important person!"

He nodded. Although George said this in his usual lighthearted tone, he looked afraid.

Lio knelt next to him. "It's going to be all right, George."

"But what if I can't stay with mum and dad? What if I can't stay with you?"

"I'll never leave you," he said, "I can't. Not after all those years, right?"

"Really?" Lio smiled again. "Of course." George nodded, his dark curls jumping, and turned to go. But he changed his mind and came back. "Lio," he said, "I think

I like you more than mum and dad."

This overwhelmed him. He thought of all those years spent without their parents, without anyone to help him in difficult situations, without anyone to understand. Except for George. He struggled on thanks to him. "Me too." he said. George laughed. He ran to him and hugged him. Lio hugged him back. In spite of his manners, interests, curls, and age George was his little brother, and closer to him than anyone else could have been.

That moment Georgiana came into the room. "Come, the cab is here." "Are we going to the airport?" asked George as he raised his bundle. "Yes." "I don't have enough money for tickets," said Lio. "But I do," responded Georgiana. "What about the spirits?"

"They'll loose our track when we'll be in the air."

"But they'll know where to find us." "We'll move on as soon as your parents join us in Iceland. It's no use for them to keep hiding from you now that you know everything." Lio nodded and they went towards the stairs. "I've always wanted to go to Iceland," said George, "that's where all the Vikings live." Lio chuckled.

Miss Rose was sitting in her armchair in the living room,

she was breathing heavily and looked pale. "You can't go to Iceland wearing this!" She pointed at their coats and boots.

"Don't worry, we'll manage," said Lio as he sat next to her.

"And poor George is all feverish…" she mumbled.

"Thank you for your hospitality, Jane," said Georgiana, then she helped George get all his things into a small bag.

"Next time I come I'll bring you a pink rose. One of those big ones you like." promised Lio and kissed her. The old lady held him for a while. "Take care of them."

"I will." With these words he dressed up and the three of them left Miss Rose's house.

***

That is the narrative which I read that night to young Trevor, and I think, Watson, that under circumstances it was a dramatic one. The good fellow was heart-broken at it, and went out to the Terai tea planting, where I hear that he is doing well. As to the sailor and Beddoes, neither of them was ever heard of again after the day on which the letter of warning was written. They both disappeared utterly and completely. No complain had been lodged with the police, so that Beddoes had mistaken a threat for a deed. Hudson had been seen lurking about, and it was believed by the police that he had done away with Beddoes and had fled. For myself I believe the truth was exactly the opposite. I think that it is most probable that

Beddoes, pushed to desperation and believing himself to have been already betrayed, had revenge himself upon Hudson, and that he fled from the country with as much money as he could lay his hands on. Those are the facts of the case, Doctor, and if they are of any use to your collection, I am sure that they are very heartily at your service.'

Lio closed the book and sighed. How he missed the ending of the <u>Gloria Scott</u>. He couldn't get himself to finish reading the story for about a year and then he had lost the book. He was sitting in the chair between Georgiana and George, who was gazing out of the window with amazement. It was George's first time in an airplane, so the view of the sky took his breath away. They were in the airplane for only about an hour, but Lio wasn't worried about the long flight that awaited them, he had a very thick book in his hands. He had taken the book after making the taxi driver stop by his house to get their passports before leaving the village.

He glanced over George's shoulder at the white clouds that surrounded them. Suddenly a strange thought entered his mind. *In the wild land of hills and ice we shall wait till we can wait no more. Every second brings the moment nearer.*

The thought wasn't his own creation, but he had hoped to hear it. With some surprise he noted that it wasn't a lyric from a song at all, but more of a line from a text. Lio knew exactly to whom the thought belonged. The thought belonged to someone he couldn't forget even after all those years, to someone, how strange it seemed, waiting for him at the end of the journey. Lio leaned back with a smile. This turned out to be his best birthday after all. He had learned the truth about his family. He had freed himself of his fears, he was going to see his parents again. At last. Lio didn't know he how would behave, what he would say, or what he would do.

But he believed he'd know in the right time. Yes, it was his best birthday. The only thing that could improve it was…

"Look, Lio," said George, "it's snowing!"

MANY WISHES

The beeping sound of the alarm clock finally ended the silence. Mary grumbled and opened her eyes. It was still dark. It was always dark at half past six. "Why does school start so early?" she murmured to herself as she got up and went clumsily out of her room; probably to the bathroom.

The picture faded and appeared again, this time in another room. I was right, she went to the bathroom. Mary was brushing her teeth and it looked as if she would fall back asleep at any moment. She finished and started to dress. I stopped the magic and the image faded again. I really didn't have to see that part. *Fine.* I took my notebook and wrote down all I had seen. Yes, it was enough.

I put the mirror I had just used on my bed side table and got up myself. A smile appeared on my lips when I realized I wasn't tired. That was a good sign, because I was almost always tired. I put on my dress and tried to tie it up. The buttons were the worst. They were on the back, so I couldn't see them and it was very hard to hold them.

I fought with it for a few minutes and then I heard the door opening. I could recognize the person who came in thanks to my ability to read some of his thoughts, so I didn't turn around.

"Wow, I'm so glad I don't have to wear clothes with buttons," said Lydia. I didn't answer. "Need some help?" she asked. I nodded. Lydia was a muse. Sometimes they were called fairies, but there was a big difference. Muses were related to people's life. They made them feel and think and fairies could not do that. Besides, fairies don't exist anymore. Muses were in a much lower class than mine, but I did adore them. They had feelings. I didn't. The only feeling I have ever felt was anger and it had appeared more and more often.

Lydia buttoned up my dress and sat down on my big bed. "So," she asked, "what are you doing? We have a long time before the lessons start."

"I did my homework. I watched a human."

"I didn't know your class has to do it too. It's really useless to you, isn't it? You don't need to observe people's lives."

"It is useless indeed. But sometimes it can be quite interesting," I smiled at her. Lydia smiled back, playing with her black hair. "And may I ask what is so interesting for you?"

"Their hobbies, their thoughts, their conflicts… their adventures."

Lydia laughed, "Why would such a pretty goddess as you need an adventure?" I shrugged.

"I'm sure you wouldn't get yourself in trouble, no matter what happens," she added.

"No, I'm too careful for that. But adventures are interesting." I said and leaned down to get my shoes. "How is Kasumi?"

"She had a headache, but now she seems to be fine."

"Fine," I said, "I'll come to see her later." I didn't say more, which was a sign for Lydia to leave. She gave me another smile and left my room.

I liked Lydia, and Kasumi too, but I just couldn't bear long conversations. They could understand that and that made them very good friends, although they were just muses. I lied on the bed again. I didn't hurry. I never hurried. I had a long time before the lessons started. Well, not exactly. The word "time" has meaning only to mortals. We immortals don't use and don't feel the time. This word is known to us just thanks to the observations we've made.

All words are actually names. A name without a meaning is not a name. A thing without a name is not a thing. A thing with a name makes both exist. But a name of a thing without a meaning is nothing. Meaning is the important part. So we immortals know the word and some of us even the thing, but not the meaning. That's why time doesn't exist. It's simple.

I was wondering if something special was supposed to happen. No, I woke up, did my homework, then I would have class, then I would visit the muses, hear people's wishes, send an angel to fulfill the wishes and then I would have time for myself. Nothing special today. I stood up. Then I looked at the room and tried to remember what I wanted to do. *Oh, yes, my notebook.*

***

The classroom was empty when I entered. It was a large, round room, the ground was covered with a soft carpet. At the center there was a round pond, leveled with the carpet that seemed to fall into the dark water. Everything stayed motionless, but the movement of the pond was always there, hidden beneath the calm surface. It was like a black hole that could take you to far, lonely places. I sat next to it and looked down, trying to find the dark bottom. It had to be somewhere.

Another young god entered and sat right next to me,

although he surely knew it made me uneasy. Then he decided to talk, although he surely knew I preferred silence.

"So, how are you, Danaë?" he said. I waited a while before I answered. "Very well," I said at last, "and you?"

"I'm quite in trouble… I spoke to a human." he added the last part just as he realized that I wouldn't ask him for the reason. I looked at him. That did annoy me. "Leuren! This is strictly forbidden."

He smiled. I noticed his eyes were bright blue. I never looked at them before. "This is all the fun. And why not answer, if people ask you questions and need your advice?"

"A god should send an angel to talk to them."

"You really think angels are the sign of our power? It only shows we gods are so lazy and we can't do anything ourselves." I did not know what to say. It was perfectly true. I suddenly realized that I understood him all this time. Leuren enjoyed my amusement. He came closer.

"Danaë, I never believed that, but now I must confess you are even more beautiful than anyone had ever told me." Anger overpowered me. I rose up and went to the other side, my head proudly raised up. *How dared he say such a thing?*

The rest of the young gods arrived and I mingled with the class before Leuren could catch me, but he wasn't that stupid anyway. When I got mad I could destroy the whole building with a single move of my finger. Then the time had come. We all felt that. We sat around the pond and closed our eyes. The lesson started.

A lesson in our world is very different from lessons in the world of humans. We don't have teachers and we don't learn. We know everything from the moment we first see the light. Our lessons are supposed to make us forget. The only thing that must stay in our minds are related to the specific god. If there had been someone who wouldn't take lessons, he would stay the ruler of everything. He would be the God.

I took a deep breath and let all my memories disappear. I had to concentrate and let the time pass…

Everything looked exactly the same when I opened my eyes. It's hard to tell how long the lessons lasted in human time. Most likely something between five minutes and five years. The young gods smiled at each other and started to leave the room. I didn't move for a long time. I was exhausted. I fell onto the pillow next to me, to try and recover my strength.

***

Water. Food. Money. Peace. Luck. Heal old people. Help the young ones. Save the forest. Hunt down animals. Stop storms. Sell. Buy. Take. Give. Kill…

"Danaë?"

"No."

"Danaë!" I forced myself to open my eyes. It was Lydia. "What?" I asked. I didn't have the temper for a talk. "I was worried, you didn't wake up for a long time and…"

"Many wishes. Hard times. People need help. Now let me finish."

"I need your help too. Are you coming or not?"

I looked at the canopy of my bed. We were in my room. I couldn't remember how I had gotten here. *Did Lydia somehow take me from the classroom? No, muses can't enter rooms for gods…*

"Are you coming?" She tried to ignore my angry look and went out. I followed her. The place we were living in was divided into three buildings. The largest one stood for gods and the other two for muses and angels. They were all connected by the main hallway, and there were a few smaller corridors that didn't go to all of the important places. Some of them were even forbidden.

We exited the biggest building. There were no changes in the gray, undecorated hallway, but I could feel it. A foreign thought entered my head. It belonged to Lydia. She was worried, but I didn't know why. I touched her hand and gave her a friendly smile. It helped a little, maybe.

After a short time we entered the Muse Building. Lydia walked first so I didn't have to concentrate on the way.

Later, I decided, I would find Casiel and give him the messages for the people. This time most of them came from a similar time period, so he shouldn't have trouble delivering them all. Every time we gods listened to wishes or watched humans we would become a little confused because of the time changes there. I would need to write everything down before I forget them all.

Doors appeared along the sides of the hallway. Lydia led us to the right one. Then we entered.

We found Kasumi sitting on a low chair and drawing. She got up and welcomed us with a smile. We all sat down.

"Any news?" I asked.

"I have a little headache, but otherwise every thing's all right," said Kasumi, pushing her blond hair behind her ears. She was quite short, with big blue, smiling eyes. Kasumi wanted to become the protector of old Japanese thoughts.

"A little headache?" cried Lydia, "She hadn't gone to class the last three days!" Lydia was always much more serious than Kasumi. They were interested in totally different things, their thoughts were different, their accents were different, they looked different. Lydia had black hair, brown eyes, and thick eyebrows. Her skin was a bit darker too.

"Could you stop it Danaë?" said Lydia, and then she added: "Please?"

"I'm fine," protested Kasumi. It was hard to decide which one was right. One was too relaxed and the second was too worried.

"Let me try," I said. I leaned forward and touched Kasumi's forehead. All her feelings entered my head at once. Then I sat back and stopped the connection. It made me tired. "No," I said, "you'll have to get over it alone." They were quiet for a while, then Lydia went to get something to eat.

Kasumi smiled again. I could see her small teeth. Suddenly a yellow liquid appeared on her front teeth and she spat it out onto a tissue. That was weird. I was getting worried too. Kasumi pretended not to see my suspicious glance. I got up and walked in circles around the low table. Kasumi watched me in silence. She was wondering if I was tired or worried, but I was both, and she probably knew why, but I hadn't confirmed any of that out loud.

Neither of us spoke until Lydia arrived. She put the food on the table and sat down. Then both of them watched me. I continued walking. It was calming. I needed to be calm. A headache was normal. It would pass quickly. *But this liquid…* I was sure I knew about it before, but I couldn't remember anything. That was the worst aspect of my lessons. I forget something, and then I know I forgot something, but I never forget that I forgot it, whatever it is. *How annoying!*

"They're waking up." It took me a short while until I realized that I was the speaker. The muses looked up at me, confused.

"Who's waking up?" The thoughts stayed in my head for a long time. I tried to get rid of them. Then I shrugged.

"What are you talking about, Danaë?" asked Kasumi.

"Was I talking?"

"Yes, you said they're waking up," this time even she didn't smile. My eyebrows rose up. "Who is waking up?"

"I don't know, that's what you said,"

"I don't remember saying anything,"

Kasumi and Lydia looked at each other, confused.

"Why would someone sleep? And why would he wake up?" I continued.

"We don't know, Danaë,"

I stopped walking. Why were we talking about sleeping if no one knew why? Lydia tried to say something, she probably didn't know how to start, because her mouth opened and closed a few times without letting any sound out. "Are you all right?" she said at last, carefully.

"Of course I am all right!"

The anger flickered and bubbled inside my body, getting closer and closer to my heart, leaving burning steps after it. The little flames grew bigger… I took a deep breath just before the fire took control of me. The air hit my lungs like cold water.

I came back to myself when the danger was over and found Kasumi and Lydia talking quietly. This was not the first time anger had almost overpowered me. I had to be very careful with it. The battle inside me hadn't taken longer than a few seconds, but I almost couldn't remember what we were talking about, or what had made me so angry. I forgot something. What did I forget? My mouth opened in a yawn. *Maybe I would remember after some rest.*

"You should sleep," I said to Kasumi, "I'll try to figure out what to do." Kasumi nodded. She was afraid of me. That made me feel lonely. No one dared to argue with me, no one was really close to me. Even my best friends were afraid of me. I nodded too and left the room. *Is loneliness the price of power?*

I went to the second small building to find my angel. This hallway was full of angels. They were talking and laughing with each other. Some of them smiled at me or said something. I tried to smile back, as I made my way through the winged crowd. At last I found Casiel standing near the big hall. I waved at him. He came to me, leaving the other angels behind.

"I need your help," I said. He answered, but I couldn't

hear him well. The hallway was too noisy. I pointed at the door to his room and he nodded. Then we entered. A sigh escaped from my mouth.

Casiel laughed. "Too noisy for you?" he provoked. I ignored him. He was the only person who dared to provoke me. He knew I wouldn't hurt him. Also, I didn't really mind. I knew he did it just because he liked me. I looked at him for a while.

Casiel was a slim young angel, not taller than me. His short, straight hair was blond, almost silver and it covered most of his forehead. He had bright blue eyes, a smile on his pink lips, a little nose and a pair of big and perfectly white wings. I dare say he was quite close to me too. Not as close as Kasumi and Lydia, of course, but close enough to talk freely with me.

"How many wishes did you receive today?" he asked.

"Many, but I didn't hear them all yet."

"Would you like me to talk to the humans?"

Leuren's voice echoed in my mind, '*You really think angels are the sign of our power? It only shows we gods are so lazy and we can't do anything ourselves.*' "Yes, I'll give you their names," I said to Casiel, casting aside the unpleasant thoughts.

I dictated the names as he wrote them down in his small notebook.

Then we went to the hallway again and continued half of the way together. When we got to the entrance of the corridor that leads to the human world, Casiel went there. This corridor was accessible only to angels. I continued straight, I never entered that corridor and I didn't want to.

Now the hallway was empty. It was nice to be alone, and so I smiled, just like that, because nobody wanted me to smile that moment. Then my legs moved quicker and quicker and I was higher and higher until I walked in the air. Every god could do this, but it was still fun, especially when no one was watching. Maybe I was shy… I didn't know.

I lowered myself and my feet touched the hard floor when the God Building began opening its doors in front of me in a slow, lazy yawn. Then I walked into my room and shut the door. My reflection watched me from the mirror on the gray wall. I stopped for a while and looked at it. My figure was just the right size, not too tall and not too short with a perfectly straight back. I was very thin and the way I held my body showed self-confidence. My face was not too round. I had light pink cheeks, big, dark eyes, a nice nose and thick pink lips that were very prominent on my pale skin. My hair was so long that it touched my knees, looking much like golden waves. I was very pretty.

Everyone here thought I would become the goddess of beauty, but I didn't want to become that. What does a goddess of beauty do? Look at her reflection and think only about herself. That wasn't my level. I was very clever, and I definitely didn't mean to forget all of my knowledge.

I broke through the distracting thoughts and came straight to the point. What is this yellow liquid? What had made me so angry? What did Lydia say? What did I say?

I walked in circles, trying to calm myself down. "Fine," I said to myself, "what can make me angry?" *When someone says I am beautiful. When someone tells me what to do. When someone doesn't believe me.* I stopped. "When someone doesn't believe me..." I said loudly, "when someone thinks I'm not all right."

'Are you all right?' Yes, that's what she asked. That's what had made me so angry. Now it was easier to concentrate on the rest of the conversation. She wouldn't have asked me if I'm all right if I hadn't said something. What did I

say? It had to be a question…

All this thinking made me tired. I wanted to sleep… *Sleep!* We were talking about sleeping. But why would someone talk about sleep? *'Why would someone sleep?'* I was surely on the right track. If someone's asleep why would he wake up? *'Why would someone wake up?'*

Now I knew. Kasumi asked me something about waking up and then these questions came. I probably said something a second before I forgot it. What did I say? Oh! Sometimes, not that often, it happened to me; that I forgot more than one memory at a time and had to somehow re-discover them. Then I would remember, but I really hated that. At last I lied on my bed, exhausted. My eyes closed but I didn't sleep. I didn't want to hear all the wishes and go look for Casiel again. I needed a rest, but that doesn't exist for gods. We knew the name, the meaning, but not the thing.

The time passed. I breathed slowly and didn't let my thoughts interrupt me.

Suddenly the door opened and Casiel flew in. He didn't knock or close the door behind him. I opened my eyes and gave him an angry look. "Don't look at me like that," he cried, "why aren't you sleeping? I should be on my way with your messages, but you didn't listen even to one wish!"

Of course, why didn't I think of that! Lydia woke me up, so I didn't hear all the wishes and now Casiel had to go again.

"I couldn't sleep, I had to do something." I tried to give my voice an angry tone. It worked, because Casiel closed the door. "Then sleep now," he commanded. My anger grew even more, but I didn't argue. I knew it was my fault. I closed my eyes. When I opened them after a short while Casiel was still standing there, looking at me. I repeated this action once more. Casiel watched me.

"I can't sleep," I said at last.

"Why not?"

"You're watching me!"

"I want to finish quickly."

"Casiel!"

 "All right," he said and sat on the chair next to my bed. It was the only high chair in my room. "Better?" I nodded and tried to fall asleep again. I could feel his stare through my closed eyelids, so I opened them. "It is not better."

"Fine, I see," he was getting angry too, "you're always tired, but only when we need you to sleep you can't." I chose not to answer.

"Close your eyes," he said and I obeyed. The room was quiet for a while and then I jumped up, amazed. Casiel was singing. It was the last thing I expected him to do. He had such a beautiful voice. My body fell on the bed and my eyes were heavy. I didn't remember the last time I was so calm. All my fears were now gone. I felt Casiel's hand touching my hair gently and I fell deeper and deeper into the world of wishes…

***

The angel was still sitting beside my bed when I woke up. I gave him my messages as quickly as I could and he finally left the room, his steps clapping hastily on the floor. He had to hurry. I didn't get up. It was the end of the day, so I had time to be alone and think.

***

The vacation started. Thomas got up at ten o'clock. His little brother was already downstairs, eating cereal. Thomas didn't mind the mess on the round table and sat down too. There was a message from their dad. He wrote that he and mum would return home late in the evening and that the boys could watch television if they wanted to. They immediately ran to it, enjoying the click of the round button below the screen as they turned the television on.

They watched their favorite show, it was about monsters, some kind of a horror film played mostly by dummies.

Suddenly, I threw the mirror down, closed my eyes and put my hands on my ears, shivering all over. The music of the film gave me a bad feeling. It stopped with my magic which had broken as the tiny mirror hit the floor and I could move again. I got up carefully, glancing at the broken mirror at my feet. *Something is going on.*

I ran out and straight to Kasumi's room, leaving my door open. I burst in and tried to find the right words to say. Kasumi looked at me, her eyes bigger than usual, searching too, for the right question. She spoke first, "What happened?"

"I don't know," I almost whispered, "but soon I'll have to find out."

"It's something in the world of humans, isn't it?"

"I don't know," if it was only in the world of humans, a muse wouldn't get ill. Muses, gods and angels nearly never got ill. The problem in the world down there must be affecting us too.

"Kasumi," I came closer and sat next to her, "tell me exactly what you feel,"

The muse was quiet for a while. She spat more yellow liquid on a tissue next to her. I couldn't tell if she knew what I was thinking about. "It's only a little headache,"

"Nothing more?"

"Not physically…" she tried not to look at me, "I am afraid." I looked at her helplessly.

"It's when you always think something bad is going to happen," Kasumi tried to explain, "and your heart beats really fast and it's hard to breath… Understand?" I didn't understand. "I'm not worried about myself," she continued, "I'm worried about Lydia, and all of my friends, and you. I was never really serious, but now I am." Then we were both quiet. It was the first time Kasumi didn't laugh when she spoke. And I couldn't understand what was happening to her.

"Don't observe the humans," I said at last.

"I must!" She was terrified of what I said.

"Now you must stop." It wasn't advice. It was a command; and the end of the talk. I didn't look for Lydia, it wasn't important right now, I didn't even go to my room. I went to the classroom, sat down next to the pond and thought. Everything was suddenly so strange, so out of control. I knew something was wrong and I knew what was important to do right then, but I didn't know why, or what it had to do with our situation. I didn't even know how I knew all that!

The pond in front of me was perfectly round. It was the first time I thought about that. It was another important point. Like a big puzzle that didn't make sense. I stayed there and thought until other gods arrived. We waited for the rest of the class, but when no one else came we started without them. This time no one interrupted me and the lesson was as usual, except for a few occasional worried glances at the door. We were all very tired when we finished, so I fell asleep the second I entered my room.

***

Money. Luck. More soldiers. Help to find a shelter. Hunt enough for food. Buy more weapons. Find secret messages. Destroy all the pagans. Only one side is right. Kill!

The last wish woke me up. I've never heard so many bad wishes from so many different time periods at once. I felt confused and dizzy as I slowly got up, rubbing my aching head. All of a sudden I knew what was happening. *War.* A war because of religion. I wrote everything down before I could forget. Then, still a little tired, I went to the Angel Building.

The hallway there was full, as usual. I tried to read the thoughts of all the angels around me, but Casiel wasn't there. I searched all the hallways unsuccessfully, so I entered his room. He wasn't there either, but I waited for him anyway. At last he came, waving his wings and pushing his silver hair out of his face. Then he stopped and looked at me. "You were very quick today," he said,

I showed him the list of wishes. A little wrinkle appeared between his eyebrows when he looked at it. Maybe he was feeling the same feeling Kasumi tried to explain to me before. "War…" he said.

I nodded. Then I started to dictate my answers to him.

"Wait, Danaë," Casiel stopped me, his tone different than usual, "are you sure you want to answer and fulfill these wishes?"

"Of course I'm sure," I felt my anger appearing inside me, "now let me continue,"

"I don't think it's a good idea,"

"But I do. And it is my duty, after all."

"Danaë, think about that."

"Why? You are not the one to decide."

"No, but I am your angel, and your choice affects me too."

Is he seriously telling me what to do? What does he think of himself? I took a deep breath. "Why is it so important to you?"

It was hard for Casiel to control himself too. "Because war is a bad thing and you can stop it if you don't fulfill these wishes."

"And why is it so bad?"

"Because people kill each other. They hurt each other and destroy their planet."

"But why does it matter to you? I kill people all the time."

"Yes, but you don't help them kill each other!"

I didn't answer for a long time. Casiel was very serious. I didn't understand him. They couldn't hurt him, so why did he mind?

"You really don't mind it, Danaë?" he asked.

"I mind only the part that causes us problems. The other is the same to me."

The angel gave me an angry look. "Their problems are our problems," he cried, "our world can't exist without the other one. You should know that! And I do mind because it's subhuman to take lives just like that!"

I didn't interrupt him, telling myself he was only tired. He knew I didn't mind it, but he went on and on, trying to explain a thing I would never understand. He rambled on until At last he stopped to catch his breath. I didn't let him continue. "Fine," I said, "I'll wait with the answers until you feel better about it." Then I turned around and opened the door. A sudden noise made me turn back. I found Casiel on the floor. I couldn't breathe. I ran to him and almost fell down next to him, touching his white wings.

"Casiel, what is it?" My voice sounded different than usual, like if it wasn't mine. It was very…nice. "What happened? Is it because of me?" The angel didn't move for a long time. I wanted to call someone to help me, but I couldn't leave Casiel alone, I didn't know why. Should I try to contact someone with magic? Or do something myself? I wasn't sure if it was the best idea…

Then Casiel sat up. He looked very tired.

"Is everything all right?" I cried in this strange voice. He nodded and got up. He stood there for a while, trying to find his balance. Then he looked at me, "I have headache," he said. Anger was all I felt that moment. *Not again!*

"I can deliver these messages, if you want to," he said

quietly. He probably thought I was angry because of our fight.

"No," this time my voice was normal and I felt much better, under control. "Wait here, I'll come soon." I was just about to open the door when he called back at me. I turned around. "Thank you," he said, grateful. This time I recognized it.

I exited, my head full of questions. *Does this human war affect us that much? Is that the reason for the illness in our world? What happened to my angel? What happened to me? How did I know what he felt?* No, this wasn't the right question. I had always known what gratefulness was, but now it was the first time I could understand the meaning.

"Gratefulness," I said out loud to the gray walls. "Gratefulness". The single word made my heart open, and my lips smile gently. It made the air clearer and the taste in my mouth sweeter. It made me feel. I stopped in my place, whispering this lovely word again and again. I liked it. I was… grateful to know it. Gratefulness.

I decided to go to my room first. Lydia and Kasumi could wait for a while. I lied on my bed and tried to figure out what to do. Kasumi was ill and now Casiel joined her.

Things were getting out of control. Something about it made me exceedingly uncomfortable. I didn't answer the wishes, life as I knew it began to fall apart as my preside schedule stopped functioning, all this because of a human war.

I wouldn't have cared it, if there weren't problems in my world too… I did only because things went out of control. I was sure it wasn't the same reason Casiel cared. I got up, sat in front of the big mirror since the small one was broken, and took a fruit from the bowl on my desk. Gods don't need to eat very much, a little once every few human weeks or months was enough, but I was hungry in that instant. My reflection copied my moves, it's pretty eyes watching mine. At last I left my room, leaving the fruit on the table.

Kasumi's room was empty, so I went to Lydia's next door. The muses stopped talking when I entered. I tried to join their conversation to forget my fears for a while. All the rooms in the Muse Building are exactly the same. It wasn't anything special, because the rooms in the Angel Building were unified too, although they looked different than the muses'. This was the same for my building as well.

Lydia was telling us about the lesson today, which looked very different from my lessons. I was glad to see Kasumi was herself again. She talked a lot, laughed and said many useless things. Lydia laughed too and they told their old jokes and sang just because it was fun. I mostly listened and smiled, sometimes uttering a sentence or two. It seemed as if we traveled back in time to before Kasumi's headaches started.

We didn't know how long we were talking. We had just let the time pass. "And how is your angel, Danaë?" Lydia asked me after a long conversation about the best side of the room to put your chair in, if you had one. I looked for the right words to describe what had happened to Casiel. I knew Kasumi nor Lydia had ever seen an angel. Only gods were allowed to visit all the buildings.

"I saw him just before I came and..." a loud siren interrupted me.

We all jumped up to this sound. I looked at the muses. They nodded. I left them and went to the hallway, walking a few inches above the ground. The siren was heard only in case of alarm, and then all the gods would have to meet in the big hall. I wasn't the first one on my way. Other gods were walking quickly just like me in the hallway. I looked back when one of them fell down. The siren sounded again, so I couldn't stop, but after a short while I saw more of them, lying on the hard floor, or slowing down with a sudden headache. At last I arrived to the hall. After a short while Leuren came to me.

"What happened?" he said.

"Don't you know? All the last wishes tell that."

"I didn't listen to wishes the last two days." This sentence made me look at him again. I saw yellow liquid on his teeth when he asked me about the wishes. I couldn't respond, different thoughts had entered my head. How come I hadn't noticed his absence during lessons? Why did so many being come down with an illness with no clear explanation? The sight in the hallway only implied that every minute there was more of them. At last Leuren asked another god and left me pondering alone. Soon everybody arrived and the assembly began.

We stood in a large circle, so close to each other that our arms almost touched. It made me very uneasy, but I knew it was the only way to let all the gods into the circle. This time there weren't only the young ones, the other gods arrived too. We all closed our eyes and listened to the thoughts. When we all heard enough we opened our eyes.

"So, the problem in our world is this mysterious illness. I guess everyone knew this even before the assembly started," said one of the oldest gods. We all nodded.

"How is it related to the human war?" asked the goddess of wind.

"They are probably fighting about us," answered a young one.

"People never understand there are no bad gods," complained the god of fire, "sometimes they fight just because someone decided to call us with another name."

"Had it been only because of us the illness wouldn't have hit the angels and muses."

"I noticed only the blue eyed beings came down with it."

This argument hushed the assembly. He's right, Kasumi, Leuren and Casiel, they all have blue eyes.

"Our duty is to stop this mess." said someone at last. He was also right, everything had to be expected again. "So we'll have to stop the war."

"We even don't know what it is about!"

"We could always ask the humans," said Leuren.

"No," cried an old god, "it is forbidden! We can only answer their questions by sending an angel. This is the rule!"

"Why not? We are the rulers!" he protested.

"It can't be changed and that's it."

The argument about the war continued for a long time. Finally, we all decided not to fulfill any wishes, instead we would only write them down for the useful information they provided. The assembly parted.

I found Kasumi and Lydia at the entrance to my building, on their part of the hallway. They both asked so many questions all at once. I tried to explain what was happening as briefly as I could. Yet, I could see they had many more questions and I didn't wait to hear them so I went to my room without another word.

It didn't make me feel any better, I walked in circles, stopping again and again. At last I raised up my mirror from the floor and cast another spell, hoping that I would be able to see through the broken glass. The image was multiplied, but it didn't matter that much. This time I saw an old man, most likely in the beginning of the Middle Ages. He was sitting on a rickety chair next to a dirty wooden table. His clothes were dull and ripped, his gray hair uncombed and his eyes tired and worried. He was leaning on the table, holding his head between his hands. I had a feeling I saw tears on his cheeks, but I couldn't be sure. I tried to see the back of the house, it had broken windows and a cloth instead of a door.

Somehow I guessed that the man was the only person living in this house. He probably didn't have any friends or family that were killed in war. So why did he cry? Maybe, I thought, the war destroyed his house. Or they wanted him to pay something? Maybe he was just sad like all people are sometimes, but I didn't think it was the only reason. This time people weren't fighting only about gods, this was certain. So what could it be? Something as strong as we immortals are, something that affected their lives.

I couldn't take my eyes off the poor man, although there was nothing I wished more in that moment. I couldn't just ignore the look in his eyes. He was surely cold and hungry, thinking only about the problem in his world. I knew none of it exactly, but I believed it with all my heart. I felt aching somewhere inside myself and tears filled my eyes. It was probably what he felt too. I pitied him, I was truly sorry. Sorry. It was noble and horrible at the same time. I was sorry.

The picture faded, the mirror fell on the floor again, and I didn't move, having no idea how to react. I couldn't control myself anymore. Suddenly, I was sorry for that too. At last I laid down, my back on the hard, gray floor, not knowing why, or for what I was sobbing and crying.

I tried to stop, but it didn't work. I never cried before. I opened my eyes in panic and forced them to look up through the tears. *Focus on the ceiling,* I commanded myself. It was gray, undecorated and even, just like all the buildings. Or was it? Did I see it only because of my unclean eyes? I wiped them and looked again. There were odd spirals and signs, all moving and changing without end. *Letters*, I suddenly understood.

'They're waking up'

I jumped up, reading the message again. Then I ran to the hallway, my head raised up, seeing that the ceiling here was covered with the same message. It was always there, but no one ever noticed. It was the answer to our questions!

I could feel my heart in my throat and I was breathing heavily. My eyes opened wider, expecting to see the wonders that appeared in my imagination. Many wishes and ideas came into my mind. Hope. Now I was running, hoping I would arrive in time. I ran, wishing I would give an end to this war, to this illness, wishing… Oh, I had so many wishes I couldn't even say what I was wishing for!

The stifling building suddenly seemed like a never ending plane with so many paths leading to different places. So many choices, so many options, and there was a chance I would find the right one. Hope.

I knew what to do now. Kasumi was in her bed, spitting liquid and trying to sleep and Lydia was in the other room. I sat beside the Muse's bed. She opened her eyes and smiled a little. Now that I knew what to expect I could see her blue eyes were turning gray We had to work quickly. "I know what is happening."

"In the world of humans?" Kasumi sounded interested.

"In both worlds."

"What?"

"I'll tell you when Lydia arrives," Kasumi was disappointed. She asked me about it a few more times unsuccessfully. "And do you mean to do something about it?" she asked at last,

"I have a plan,"

"What plan?" "I'll tell you when Lydia arrives."

She gave me an angry look and tried to get more information from me, but I waited. We didn't wait too long, Lydia was glad to see me. She sat on the other side of the bed and I told them my idea. They didn't seem to like it at all, but I knew it would be their reaction.

"It's too dangerous," this was Lydia's first thought.

"It is less dangerous than letting Kasumi just sit here."

"This time I agree with Lydia," Kasumi said, "what could be more dangerous than to enter a forbidden corridor?"

"Trust me. I don't want to frighten you."

"Frighten me?" Kasumi jumped out of the bed, "what is happening to me, Danaë? I must know!"

I waited for a long time. It was hard to tell her. I was sorry for Kasumi. "I still have to make sure," I said.

"And this corridor is the only way?" Lydia said. I nodded.

There was silence. This time I respected the muses and didn't read their thoughts. It was a hard situation for all of us. Kasumi and Lydia looked at each other in agreement. "It just wouldn't work, Danaë."

I got up, "Fine, then I'll go alone." With these words I exited. Kasumi ran after me.

"Danaë, why are you doing this?" she asked, "Is it because of me?" I saw tears in her eyes.

"No. It's for all of us. Your illness would affect the healthy beings too."

"Why?" she cried.

I knew she wouldn't let me go without telling her. It was her right, after all. "You are turning into someone else," I whispered, "someone with no heart." She froze. Then she started to laugh. *How childish!* Hot fire burned me inside. The air itself turned heavier.

"I can't be someone else," she said after a while, playing with her hair. "Right?" she added when she saw how I looked at her.

"It was only a joke right, Danaë?" This time she was frightened. I looked at her again. Then I went away, leaving her behind. She wanted me to tell her, I did. From now on it was her problem.

My next stop was Casiel's room. I wanted to share my plan with him too. He wouldn't react like the muses. Maybe he could even help me.

My angel listened to me in amazement, and I told him every detail of what I knew and what I didn't know. "So

I'm turning into a monster," he laughed a little, but I knew he believed me.

"Not a monster…"

"A creature with no heart is a monster, what else could it be?" he interrupted me, rubbing his little nose, "oh, well, let's not talk about that part. So you want to stop it?"

I confirmed.

He watched me for a long while. "I've never thought you would mind such a thing, and I didn't even dream you would do something about it," he said, smiling, "you've changed, Danaë."

"Do you think I should do it?" I asked quietly.

"Would I go with you?"

"Maybe," Casiel looked down at the table. "I've always wanted to see what was in this corridor," he said at last, "I just never thought of doing a forbidden thing."

"So?"

His smile widened. "I'm with you."

***

The entrance was dark. I couldn't believe I was doing this. I stopped before I took the last step to the forbidden corridor. *Why was I entering? Why did I mind?* Danaë would never think of such things. But Casiel was right. I've changed. The corridor was open, with no sign to stop you, no locked door, and no red line. It was just forbidden. *Forbidden by who?* I said to myself. We gods are the rulers, no one could overpower us. I stepped forward. I entered.

The walls were getting darker and this hallway had no light. The buildings were always lit, I had never seen darkness before. I looked up, re-assuring myself that the message was on this ceiling too. It was there. It told me what was happening to the ill beings and the first step of my dangerous journey. I was just about to find out the rest of it. The light was now so far I could hardly see the few doors along the sides of the short corridor. I counted, one, two, three, four, five… and the last one. It took me a while to find the door knob. Then I went in.

I couldn't see anything but darkness. I had an odd stomachache, as if there was a bug inside, flying and buzzing, disturbing me, but it also tickled in a nice way. I hated it, but in the same time I wanted it to continue, my eyes opened wider. Curiosity. I was curious to know what would happen next, what would I find, what would I see. Curiosity.

Little by little my eyes adjusted to the gloom. I saw a square shaped object, it was large and flat, its color black and gray. It didn't move, or make any sound or light. Nothing. I came closer, the fly in my stomach buzzing, until I stood before the strange thing. The square wasn't the whole object, now I noticed there was a little rectangle with buttons on the table next to it, and many thin black ropes on the back of the square. I touched it, then I quickly took my hand back. It didn't hurt me.

So, I said to myself, *this is a computer.* The only possible way for gods to communicate with the mortals. It was one of their biggest inventions, so complicated and delicate. I never dreamed I would see one. This machine was forbidden.

"Wake up, computer, tell me what I need to do next," my magic was pouring into the black square as I said these powerful words. Nothing happened. "Hear me, computer, and obey my command."

Nothing. I tried a few more times, using all my power while losing my strength. At last I fell on the dark floor, exhausted and full of rage This rude thing wanted too much. I would teach it a lesson when it awakens. I scrambled to my feet and left the corridor. The door slammed behind me.

***

"So?" Casiel jumped out of his room when he heard me approaching. This time the hallway was empty. I waited with the answer until we entered his room and closed the door.

"So," he asked again, "what was there? Did you find the right door?"

"Yes,"

"Did you find this computer?"

"Yes,"

Casiel had a glint in his eyes. "Did you find out what to do next?"

"No…"

He stopped, giving me a strange look. "Why not?"

"It didn't wake up,"

The angel didn't move, I continued, "I used all my powers, it just didn't work." He stood there for another while. Then he started to laugh. "What's so funny?" I was angry. He knew he was crossing the line, I was about to lose my temper any moment. Casiel tried to speak, but he couldn't stop laughing. At last he fell on his bed, giggling and holding his stomach. I didn't move, keeping my hands on my chest until he calmed down.

"You didn't know how to turn the computer on?" he

gasped and giggled again. Then he got up. "Come on, I'll do it for you." I tried to forget my pride and followed him. He knew which corridor it was, because I had told him before, but when we arrived he stopped and looked back at me. "Go on!" I whispered.

Casiel smiled. He looked so full of energy, ready for everything. Excitement. Now I could feel it, there was a secret in the darkness of the corridor, a secret waiting just for us. I wasn't curious anymore, I knew what is in there, but I wanted to see it once more, to see what would happen. I enjoyed doing a forbidden thing. I was excited. Excitement.

Our steps were unusually loud in the silence. I pointed at the last door. He entered and closed the door behind me. Then Casiel froze, staring at the unknown machine on the table. At last I had to push him a little so he would go on. He came straight to the computer, looked at it as if he was looking for something and then pushed a button on the big square-standing part of the machine.

Suddenly the square was lit with blue light and many little drowned squares appeared inside it.

A surprised, little cry escaped me. *How did he do that?* He used no words, no magic, nothing!

Casiel laughed again. I've never seen him smile like that before. "This is how you turn it on," he pointed at the button he pushed before. I came closer, still all shivering from the shock.

"Where's the message?" I asked.

He suppressed another giggle. "It doesn't know what you want just like that, it doesn't think. We have to find it out by ourselves."

"So why do we need this thing?" My anger was growing bigger.

Casiel didn't listen to me. He pushed another button and the square changed its color.

"Every computer is connected to Internet. It's a system that connects billions of networks from all over the human world. We could find answers to almost every question we ask."

"Did gods give it all the answers?" I had a feeling we didn't.

"People did."

People. Each knows just a few things, but when all of them put their knowledge together they could answer every question. So why do they keep asking the gods? In the meantime Casiel opened this magical answer-giving machine. "What's your question?"

"What is the war about?" Somehow he wrote the question down, transferring it onto the screen and after a while found the answer. "It's a usual conflict about gods. Some believe in some of them and others in the others…"

"Believe?" I interrupted him, "do you mean they just believe in us?"

Casiel nodded.

"So they don't actually think we exist!"

"Of course they do," he protested, "they believe."

"But they are not sure. There's a big difference!" Casiel didn't argue with me, and returned to the computer. "It can't be a usual conflict," I continued, "immortals are becoming other beings. It must be because of the war."

The angel stopped pushing buttons and stepped back from the machine. It turned black again. Just a metal square. Casiel leaned on one of the walls. He was shivering again. I froze at this look. "Casiel?"

I repeated his name once more before he looked back at me. He was terrified. It was not the right time for him to speak, so I read his thoughts. Now it was clear. A lot of people believed some of us, immortals, were monsters. There were still some that didn't think so, that was the reason for the illness.

Fire ignited my mind. The hot flames danced, moved, burned everything. They found their way out of my body, pouring from my fingers like a golden mist, creeping on the floor like poisoned snakes, licking the walls like wild beasts. The fire lit the room, and the walls that were darker than night were now deathly white.

"They are turning a human war into a war of gods." *How could they?* We are the rulers. We have the answers. We have all the powers. We have the right to give lives, to take lives. How could they? I will show them what I think about it. Me, not Casiel.

I took a deep breath. The fire cooled down, the flames soaked into the walls. Blackness came returned and cooled the white hot walls. It was impossible to see through the shadow. My angel could see me only thanks to the remains of fire on my fingertips. I walked in the air to my room. It was quicker. Casiel flew after me, but was careful not to come too close to me. All my strength left me when we entered. I stood in the middle of the room, my tired hands beside my body. The only noise was a heart beating. Was it mine or Casiel's?

I was lying on the bed. My eyes were closed. My chest moved up and down, up and down.

"Don't sleep," It was the angel. I almost didn't recognize his voice. It was trembling, less resolute, not as usual. I remembered that Kasumi always called Casiel's kind of voice cheerful. Now it wasn't cheerful at all. "They don't need you to hear their wishes." *'Not if they think my angel is a monster'*. I knew it was what he thought, but he didn't say it out loud. "Don't sleep, Danaë, not now."

He didn't want me to leave him. I opened my eyes. Casiel waved his wings a little. It was hard for him. But for me too. "Leave me alone, Casiel." He hesitated, but then left the room. I fell back. I was too tired to sleep. All I wanted was to forget everything. Thoughts about Casiel interrupted me again and again, no matter how hard I tried to get rid of them. He surely felt horrible. It was very mean to leave him in such a situation. But why did I mind? It wasn't like me at all.

Suddenly I jumped up. It was the time for a lesson. I didn't sleep like usual, so I forgot! I ran to the classroom and arrived just in time. A lot of places were empty. I sat down. We closed our eyes. This was my chance to forget, to get out of this trouble. Who knew what would I forget now?

People.

Suddenly it hit me. People knew. People made beings ill, they made us who we are, they forbade us talking to them, they made us live in this closed prison since the beginning of time and will keep us here until the end of time. I couldn't let myself forget. They want gods to rule, so we will rule. I got up. The others looked at me uncomprehendingly.

"I'm sorry," I found myself saying, "but to forget is not my decision." Then I left. Only then I understood what I had done. I decided not to forget, to open my heart to feelings, to cancel all prohibitions, to rule myself. I had to become the Goddess. After all, who said it had to be a God?

I was running, not knowing where. Every place was now mine, a tiny part of my endless kingdom. Audacity. I wasn't limited anymore, no rules could chain me. I controlled the world, I controlled myself and I didn't doubt my abilities. Audacity.

A silent voice brought my attention back to reality. It was

calling my name. It belonged to Lydia, the muse. Kasumi was standing next to her. The way they looked at me was different than before. They feared me, they loved me, they adored me. I wondered if they knew what had just happened to me, my decision and behavior. The answer was hidden and I couldn't read it from their thoughts. "We discussed what you said for a long time," said Lydia,

"And we won't let you do it alone." finished Kasumi.

"Even a Goddess needs some help." declared Casiel as he stepped forward. He stood next to the muses. They ignored all the known rules. For me. A smile appeared on my lips and I said words I had never said before; "Thank you."

***

"So you will go to world of humans, Casiel will navigate you and we will take care of our connection with you, so we can communicate," Lydia finished the discussion. The four of us were in Kasumi's room, making a plan. My role was to go to the mortals, show them that there are gods, angels and muses, and tell them that none of us were against them. The only problem was how to get back here, I had to trust Casiel.

"How many times have you been there?" Kasumi said, "Are you sure you know exactly the way Danaë would take?" He assured her that he did. I myself said little. I was all tense, biting my lips and playing with my hair. Stress. My heart was beating rapidly. It was annoying. Stress. What if I wouldn't find the way back? What if humans would make me a monster too? What if I forget something again? What if it won't be me in the other world?

This thought was the worst. Stress.

The others weren't very light headed either, except for Kasumi, of course. She laughed about every sentence, jumped around the table, sitting down and then jumping right back up again, nothing could calm her down.

"When will you go?" she asked before Lydia could add anything.

"In a little while, to arrive when it's still dark in their world,"

"I'll check it on the computer, and call you in time." promised the angel as he got up. He stopped to cough up some liquid, keeping his blue eyes on me, then he took some more tissues with him and went away.

I raised a ring from the table to store away a few recent memories. "Here," I gave it to Lydia, "now you can contact me wherever I am. Just call my name and I will hear you. Don't lose the ring!" "Don't worry," smiled Kasumi and I left them.

I stood in my room and looked at it in order to remember just in case I won't come back: Grey walls, grey floor, grey ceiling with a message on it, a bed with a canopy, table with a mirror and a little grey wardrobe. I opened it, looking for a dress with no buttons. Only one was to be found. It was blue and undecorated, but I put it on. One could never know when he would need to dress up with no Lydia to help him. After I finished I lay on my bed and rested.

Kill. Save. Hurt. Help. Curse. Bless. Forget. Remember. Give up. Hold on. Lose. Win.

"Danaë,"

I jumped up. It was Casiel's voice in my mind. "It's time."

"I'm ready, are you next to the computer?" I glanced at my room one last time before I closed the door.

"No, I know the way, we don't need it anymore. Go to the entrance to the angel building."

I obeyed with a quick pace.

"Are you there yet?"

"Yes." I could see the corridor. I've seen Casiel going there many times. It was on my right.

"OK. Turn right. No! Sorry… Turn left."

"But the corridor is on my right side."

"There's another one. Can you see it?"

"Yes…"

"So it's this one."

I hesitated, but did as he said. The corridor was very narrow, my hands brushed against the walls as I continued walking. It led only forward and it was so long that I couldn't see the other side behind me. I walked for a very long time. Casiel didn't say anything, and I was alone. I felt something on my face, it moved my hair and caressed my face with a cold, unseen hand. It was hard to decide whether this feeling was nice or annoying, but it was stronger and stronger.

Suddenly, the corridor stopped and I found myself staring into complete darkness. The air was chilly, the unknown hand raised my hair and danced with it around my face, caressing and pinching me. Then I knew, it was the wind; It was so… different to breathe it.

A flame from my hand helped me look at this odd place. There was nothing, no hallway, no path, nothing to step on. I leaned forward to see if there was something under the wind. There was a rough, dark floor, very far away from my feet. *Ground.* And the place in front of me – it was a chasm.

"Danaë, do you hear me?" Casiel returned to me.

"Yes."

"Are you at the end of the corridor?"

"Yes I am at the… edge."

"Great. Now don't worry, you'll have to fly to the other side. Go only straight, don't look down, or behind you and it will be fine. Understand?"

"Is there another side?" I asked, a little angry.

"The other world, of course. Go only straight and it will be fine. Call me if you need me."

"All right."

"Promise?"

He was really worried about me. It made me smile. "Promise." And I took my first step into the air of the real world. Walking in the air is faster than on the floor, or on the ground, but I wasn't sure if I could do it longer than I had ever tried before. The fire died out and there was nothing but darkness. My moves were perfectly coordinated, weight on one leg, then on the other leg. One, two, one, two. My breathing was regular, I didn't wink, I didn't think. I just went on.

The silence filled my ears like cotton and emptied my mind like a big magnet pulling everything away. Away.

A sharp sound woke me up from this trance. "Danaë stop!"

"Lydia!" I cried.

"Are you still in our world?"

"No,"

"Then you must come back immediately!"

"Why? I can't, I'm in the middle of nowhere and I must continue if I don't want to get lost."

"You are lost, turn around and come back!"

"What do you mean? Casiel knows the way," I got stressed again.

"He doesn't know. Kasumi suddenly fainted so I ran to Casiel for help, but he didn't remember me. I asked him where you're going and he said it's the way to the other world. Not the world of humans! His eyes were grey, Danaë!"

I couldn't breathe. Cold sweat covered my hands. My eyes were dry. Fear.

"Kasumi is waking up," Lydia continued, "oh! Her eyes are gray too! Danaë I need you! You're going to kill yourself if you don't come back!"

They're waking up.

"I can't!" I said in a choked voice. There was silence for a while.

"I locked Kasumi in my room, I'll be all right. Where are you?"

"Nowhere!" I cried, "there is no ground under my feet, nothing nearby!"

"Then stop at the first stable place you reach and come back the same way. Don't listen to Casiel! Quick!"

"I'll try."

"Thanks."

Lydia left me and I was alone again. My legs were heavy, so heavy. I didn't know if I even continued walking and I didn't care. I was afraid. A tear fell on my face and then another one. I didn't wipe them. Words and sounds escaped my lips, I didn't know what I said. My heart hurt. Fear wasn't the only thing I felt that moment. Sadness.

Kasumi and Casiel were my best friends, we had known each other ever since we knew ourselves, I knew their biggest secrets and they knew mine. They were always there to help me when I needed them, they were on my side when the others weren't, and never left me, even when I got angry. They liked me and I… I liked them. But now all this was gone. There was no Casiel to tease me. No Kasumi to laugh with, no angel and no muse. I cried and cried until I couldn't go on, my strength left me and I fell down, down, not knowing where.

***

A rough wall stood behind me, proudly showing its indifference. The top of it was too far to be seen, hidden in the black ceiling, above the sky. The chilly air left a horrible taste in my mouth. A noise could be heard somewhere above me, like a huge drum thundering, shaking the cold land.

The rocky ground I was lying on was wet, an intense chill

filled my bare arms, my eyes were open, but I couldn't see, I wasn't hurt, but I couldn't move.

It was hard to breathe, hard to think.

So this was the price of the ability to feel. Then I knew I was hurt. From inside.

"Don't leave me alone,

Oh, help me now, please,

My friends are gone,

My love turned into disease,"

Who was I talking to? I couldn't tell. I was looking to the sky, to this never-ending curtain. What could hide behind it? "Bring them back to me, bring me hope."

I'd heard these sentences many times. They were often accompanied by music, tears, or smiles, and they were talking to me. It was a prayer. But I was the one who should hear prayers!

I jumped up, breathing heavily. I didn't understand.

Who could hear a goddess's prayer? Was there another God? Was I a Goddess at all? What is a God?

I ran upwards with a cry of anger and surprise, pushing the air away from me. Up, to the sky where Gods were supposed to be. Was the god building in the sky too? I didn't know.

Who would dare to take my role, who would make a silly doll out of me? Who could get me rid of all hard decisions, of all difficulties? Who could overpower my anger, who could ever be able to win my love and trust? Is there such a person? A being stronger than me? Is there a God?

I reached the sky, entered the clouds. I doubled my speed, in hope attempting to break away from my aloneness. I slowed with fear of the unknown, and then ran again in an attempt to forget my duties. I wanted to know there was someone greater than me, someone who could protect and help me, someone who knew better than me. I would give him my life, I would be his.

My hands reached into the atmosphere, the clouds lowered and I was in the sky. It looked like a narcotic liquid, and the look of it made me thirsty, but I could not touch it, I could not drink.

I went on and on, searching for the addicting unknown.

But the sky was deserted.

I searched and searched for the beverage that could heal my heart, looked for the light that could blind me forever. Unsuccessful I let myself lower again, until the clouds surrounded me.

They looked so soft and warm. Suddenly, I realized how tired I was. I held out my hand, stretched my fingers, but they cut through the mist without a trace. The cloud was there, but I was unable to touch it. Then I knew. Gods can't be reached, they can't be seen, or felt. Gods exist in the mind, only if you believe.

When people believed Kasumi and Casiel were monsters, they turned into monsters. When people believed we lived in those closed buildings, we did so. If they stopped believing completely we would just vanish, like fairies did. Every step we made, every thought that passed our minds, was planned and controlled. Who knows who planned this journey of mine? ...*People of course.*

My cry cut through the thick air, tears filled my eyes. Fire changed the color of the sky to red and orange, golden flames and white smoke.

But this time I knew that all this anger, all this power wasn't really there. Beings passing by below would see only the dark sky. People would change my feelings and it would stop. I could feel whatever I wanted now, but these weren't real feelings. I wasn't real.

I stopped using my magic and fell, because I knew it wouldn't hurt me, and I lay, invisible, on the ground and cried without tears, without sounds. If it hadn't darkened I would still be lost in my own thoughts. Then the change of light drew me back to reality, or at least to what was the reality for me. I still didn't know if anyone except myself could see what I saw or think what I thought and in that moment I found that it didn't matter that much. I had to move, to wake up, I had to survive. Because what I saw when I raised my head was dangerous. *To me, at least.*

The cliff vanished and the sky changed to total blackness. Water filled the ground and made a muddy mass. Low bushes could be seen here and there, but they were all bare with sharp twigs.

Mud covered my hair and hands as I got up. My heart was beating quickly. Fear again. The place seemed gloomy and dark, but somehow familiar. It looked like an old picture from my memory that had been forgotten for centuries. I knew I had to get away, it was too dangerous here. But why? I couldn't remember.

"Danaë,"

The voice in my head reminded me. *Casiel.* My stomach ached. *Don't listen to him*, I repeated to myself, *calm down and don't listen!* "Danaë," his voice was usual, beautiful and familiar. I was used to it. It was hard to ignore. "I know you can hear me, Danaë." I fixed my eyes on the ground and started playing with my hair. "Listen, this place is dangerous, and there is only one way to get out. I understand you don't want to talk to them anymore?"

I started singing the first song that came to my mind. I raised my head proudly… And saw a person standing in front of me. It was a little blurred within the gloom. The only visible part of this creature were its dark gray eyes. *They woke up.*

My spine shivered. I had to get out. I turned the opposite direction, trying not to make any sudden moves. There was another silhouette, and another little group of them on my other side. I passed quickly and continued forward. There were more of them with each step, I went on slowly, trying to appear calm. Even if I wanted to run I couldn't because of the deep mud, which at this point reached my knees. All the gray eyes looked at me, dead and empty. I realized in horror that I knew this place, and I knew that I could belong here amongst them any moment now. Had my eyes looked like that when I was unable to feel?

"Don't look at their eyes and go on! Turn right when you reach a big round stone." *No*! I wouldn't fall into this trap. I continued with my head raised up and tried to recite my song quietly. The monsters didn't try to catch me. This scared me more than the worst fears my imagination could create.

"Danaë, stop! Don't look at them!" The crowd thickened. There was hardly enough place to move. *Grey eyes, dark faces...* "Please..." Casiel's voice was hopeless. "I know I am one of them now,"

Dark bodies, faded hands...

"But I can still save you,"

Mud reached my chest. Just a little farther and I'd sink. "Trust me, Danaë, as you did before."

I stopped, my eyes full of tears. I nodded, looked down to the mud, and waited for his orders. Then I felt a pair of hands holding me and raising me up from the dirt until my feet were above the ground and he carried me away. I looked only down. Now I saw the dark figures and the round stone where we turned right. I saw that all the figures were actually moving slowly in big circles. Circles.

"Don't look at the eyes," it was Casiel's voice whispering in my ear. All my self-control was gone at once. I cried, because I saw how miserable people made us and I laughed because Casiel was now with me, helping me. He could not be a monster if he still thought about me and didn't forget.

At last his hand left me and he said something more, but I didn't understand him. I looked up.

There he was. His small nose, slim hands, fair hair and wings, but his eyes were colorless. Two dark holes, for a soul without feelings is empty.

But my soul wasn't. I felt my heart beating stronger than ever, I couldn't breathe, I couldn't take my eyes off him. His beauty was now gone, but for me he was still the most beautiful person I knew.

Love. I loved his concern for me, I loved his thoughts, I loved his face, nose, wings, I loved him for who he really was and I didn't care if he were a monster or not.

Now I knew why Casiel was always by my side, listening to all my commands and bearing my anger without a word. He loved me. Once. I wanted to run to him, to caress him, and to tell him everything was all right again, but his eyes reminded me he could not love me back any more.

"Casiel, my angel," I cried, "come with me, hold my hand and I'll fulfill your wishes. Come back and everything will be all right." His pale lips moved to form a sort of smile; he slowly raised his hand. I raised mine, leaning towards him. I stretched my fingers, closed the gap between us…

Suddenly everything vanished and darkness parted us.

***

Low tunes ended the silence. They were repeated in different orders, once, twice, then a voice accompanied the notes. Little by little, sunshine lit the place and I saw a large chapel.

There were two lines of wooden chairs, all facing me, lit by the dim, colorful light from the decorated windows. Above the last line of chairs stood a great organ and a singer, the makers of the music. After a second look I noticed the room was full of beings, sitting on the chairs, praying.

They didn't have wings, they all looked quite similar, and it didn't seem as though they had any powers, although they were different from muses. I could feel their presence, their very prominent presence and they looked more…real. These were people.

People…

What am I doing here? It suddenly confused me. *How did I get to the real world?* A moment ago I was still standing face to face with a monster, a monster who was once my angel. I felt choked, I could hardly stop the tears. I almost got him back, I almost saved him, when something stopped me. And we were so close.

People.

Here they were, praying to God, forgetting their problems and making God more and more of them, problems without solution. Here they were, mighty and selfish. I didn't want to hear their prayers any more, but I didn't have an option. Their rules bound me like chains. My eyes examined each face and anger grew inside me. I hated them for what they did to me, for what they did to all beings, for their stupid rules, their stupid ideas. I did not hide my anger from them.

But… when I looked at their faces closely I saw that they were blind too. People actually believed I existed to help them according to my own will. Then how come it wasn't true? Was there any one, from any side, who knew the whole truth? Do gods control people, or do people control gods?

Now the ground under my feet felt even less stable than before. Another look at this place:

Chairs, organ, windows. People – each wearing different clothes, each having a different face, a different figure. I – standing on a stage facing the chapel. I was their Goddess, they were my Gods.

I took a deep breath. This was crazy. Disordered. I felt I was going crazy too. Everything I knew was destroyed, there was nothing I could trust now. I could forget everything and start all over again and no one would even notice.

A smile appeared on my lips. *Why not?* I jumped down and walked proudly out of the cold, gloomy room. Some people looked at me as I left, but I'm not sure whether they saw me or not.

I exited, keeping the smile on my face. I ignored all my feelings, all rules, to discover at last the secret system of all worlds.

The chapel led outside to a large, flat path under a clear night sky. Many big, unnatural machines which I recognized as cars rolled along the streets, beeping and flashing as they moved. The chilly air had a disgusting smell of gum that reached everywhere as it was being carried by a light breeze. I remained rooted to my place for a moment, not knowing where to go or what to do. The path didn't lead anywhere. Each car looked different and went in different directions. It looked like one big mess. There was no way to cross the street, so I gathered my courage and walked up, using the sky as a bridge. From up there I saw a whole maze of such roads and cars and blinking lights.

I forced myself to stare at the higher buildings that reached me, the sight below seemed to spin and fade into itself, aiming to drown me the moment I reach the unstable ground. It was the first time I saw a building from the outside. Compared to the open sky these blocks looked so ugly, uninviting, uncomfortable. I thought of Lydia, the only important thing I had in that prison I had left. *I'll get her out,* I decided, *and we'll never come back again.*

I dove and searched for all that I hadn't seen yet, looking for answers. There were people, using machines without limits, talking to anyone they liked, going anywhere they wanted, moving around the city, doing what they liked.

All kinds of people, all together, with no special rights or separation. They were equal.

I, too, entered and exited. I touched the furniture, machines, walls, talked to the people, and sang to the sleeping children although no one noticed I was there. Suddenly my eyes met my own reflection, standing in a mirror. People passed by and I saw them too, their rough hands, uneven bodies, curved smiles. I was perfect. So beautiful. Too beautiful. It almost scared me.

My white skin, my dark eyes, golden hair…

These uncommon beings could not see how perfect and different I was. They walked on, ignoring their own reflections. A few men passed by, a mother with a baby and a group of children, and old gentlemen with their wives. I forced myself to go on, entering a small room. For some reason I couldn't see the colors on the walls, recognize the furniture, or notice the trees behind the window. I could recognize a dim silhouette of a person sitting in the middle of the invisible mist surrounding me. I saw the person and a large, flat, square shaped object. It was the computer. Step by step I came nearer, my eyes fixed on the glowing screen. Suddenly I knew this person wasn't like the others, he could see me, he could feel my presence. When I got close enough, I understood he was writing.

'The angel stopped pushing buttons and went farther from the machine. It turned black again. Just a metal square. Casiel leaned on one of the walls. He was shivering.'

I froze with horror. Was I dreaming? No, gods never dream, we know the name, the meaning, but not the thing. Against my will I continued reading as the letters appeared on the screen one by one.

'Fire ignited my mind. The hot flames danced, moved, burned everything.'

I took a deep breath, trying to calm myself down, but couldn't. Every single word that flashed across the screen was true, recreating my own experience so precisely that I had to admit it to myself. *He's writing about me.*

'The fire lit the room, and the walls that were darker than night were now deathly white. "They are turning a human war into a war of gods."

I didn't understand. How could he feel my presence? How could he know what had happened to me? How could he know what I was thinking about in that moment? Was it my experience in the first place? What if it wasn't? I felt pain, somewhere inside, and fell, crying, on the floor. All my feelings attacked me at once, happiness, gratefulness, hope, curiosity, love, audacity, anger, sadness, fear, stress, surprise, regret, helplessness. Here he was, the creator of all my sufferings and happiness. Sitting next to his made-up subordinate, watching its made-up pain and hearing its imaginary sobbing through a set of shiny letters, dancing across a meaningless, lifeless object. I did not wish him to stop my pain, I did not want anything of him, I just felt overwhelmed.

Helplessness and regret and surprise and stress and fear and sadness and anger and love and hope and gratefulness and happiness and…

-   All right, sorry Danaë. I guess it was too much this time. How about this: -

The trees whispered and moved, talking with the blowing wind. Moss and mushrooms covered the wet ground and the nice smell of wood filled the quiet atmosphere. I sat down, enjoying this peaceful moment. Kasumi exited the small cottage behind my back and joined me with a cup of cold water in her hand. We loved this place, mostly because we had lived here all our lives, together, just me, Kasumi, Lydia and Casiel. Although we explored all our side of the forest, we still had a lot to learn about this place, so we didn't even think of leaving.

"Danaë, will you please clean up the bedroom? Your dresses are all on the floor," said Lydia's voice from inside. "Oh, quiet!"

"No, don't tell me what to do!" I sighed and went inside. Lydia took my place next to Kasumi. I found Casiel in the bedroom, playing on the computer. I tidied the clothes and put on my pink dress. The buttons were the worst. They were on the back, so I couldn't see them and it was very hard to hold them. "Want some help?" asked Casiel. "No." He ignored my answer and tied me up, not avoiding his chance to tickle me. I tickled him back and pushed him outside, laughing.

"I want to remember this spring," I explained. He nodded, leaning his back on the wall. "Remember. Don't forget."

Where is the end of the story, you ask? This is it, because this is the life I wished for, as a goddess. One can't know if I was the one to fulfill my own wish, because wishes can be fulfilled by everyone.

People believe in gods to make them real. Gods listen to people to and know they are real.

What is a god? A name. All words are actually names. A name without a meaning is not a name. A thing without a name is not a thing. A thing with a name makes both exist. But a name of a thing without meaning is nothing.

Meaning is the important part. This meaning exists thanks to imagination. So there are gods, muses, and angels, just like there are men and women. You, dear reader, can be sure of your existence.

And I – I am a character in a story.

Tiana Or-Gordon

A Good Snowy Winter

ACKNOWLEDGMENTS

Writing A Good Snowy Winter was the most difficult and most wonderful thing I have experienced in my life. I had no idea what I was getting into when I started writing the stories, which were at first as mysterious to me as to my characters. Slowly, my simple ideas began to develop and grow, revealing to me more and more not only about the stories themselves, but also about the world I live in and about myself. Just like these ideas, I had to develop and grow in order to continue writing, reading, and rewriting the stories, a task that turned out to be much more difficult than it had seemed at first, and which I would have surely failed without the great support I had.

First of all, I'd like to thank my good friends Kačka Matějovcová and Agáta Motlochová for listening to my stories, persuading me not to give up on them and giving me some great advice and feedback, and of course for Agáta's wonderful illustrations.

I thank my sister Anika for setting a wonderful example for George and saving the stories from becoming boring and melancholy with her positive attitude and occasional jokes, my English teacher Tyler Bush for revealing my passion for writing (in other words, my identity…), my editor Fritz Rickhoff for taking such interest in the stories, for all the help with grammar and the plots, and for making all our meetings so enjoyable, Kačka Kvapilová, Erin Louise Jones, and Sylvia Hulejová for all their help, and of course my parents, for supporting me in all I do (even if it means I spend my entire weekends behind the screen of the computer), and for doing everything it takes to make my dream of publishing this book come true.

I also thank you, the readers, for sharing the adventures with Idunn, Lio, and Danaë.

Thank you all!

Tiana Or-Gordon, November 2017